MARY ANNE AND THE HAUNTED BOOKSTORE

**Other books by
Ann M. Martin**

Leo the Magnificat
Rachel Parker, Kindergarten Show-off
Eleven Kids, One Summer
Ma and Pa Dracula
Yours Turly, Shirley
Ten Kids, No Pets
Slam Book
Just a Summer Romance
Missing Since Monday
With You and Without You
Me and Katie (the Pest)
Stage Fright
Inside Out
Bummer Summer

THE KIDS IN MS. COLMAN'S CLASS series
BABY-SITTERS LITTLE SISTER series
THE BABY-SITTERS CLUB mysteries
THE BABY-SITTERS CLUB series
CALIFORNIA DIARIES series

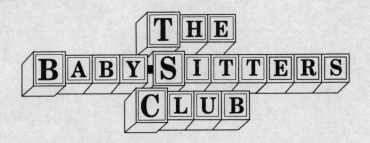

MARY ANNE AND THE HAUNTED BOOKSTORE

Ann M. Martin

AN
APPLE
PAPERBACK

SCHOLASTIC INC.
New York Toronto London Auckland Sydney

Cover art by Ed Acuña

ISBN 0-590-05974-2

12 11 10 9 8 7 6 5 4 3 2 1   8 9/9 0 1 2 3/0

Printed in the U.S.A.   40
First Scholastic printing, April 1998

*The author gratefully acknowledges
Vicki Berger Erwin
for her help in
preparing this manuscript.*

MARY ANNE AND THE HAUNTED BOOKSTORE

CHAPTER 1

I looked up from my book and listened carefully. Outside the windows all I saw were gray skies and rain. All I heard was drip, drip, drip. Or was that all? It seemed as if there might be another noise, something I could feel as well as hear. I strained to pinpoint the source, wanting to know for sure, but it seemed as if it came from everywhere.

Was it rain or the sound of a beating heart?

I shut the book I'd been reading, as if the sound were coming from inside it. The *sound* wasn't, but the idea of the sound of a beating heart had come directly from the story I'd just finished, "The Tell-Tale Heart," by Edgar Allan Poe. In the story, the main character murders an old man because he doesn't like the man's eye (it was the eye of a vulture, according to the killer). After the man is dead, the killer hides the body under the floor. The police come to search the house, because a neighbor

1

reported a strange noise. The killer is so sure that the police won't be able to detect any evidence of the murder that he tells them to sit in the dead man's bedroom, directly over the spot where he'd hidden the body. But then he hears the sound of a beating heart, and it beats louder and louder. Finally, it grows so loud that the man is sure the police are making fun of him by pretending not to hear. He confesses to his crime, because of the beating of the victim's "hideous heart."

Now, why had I, someone who can't listen to ghost stories in broad daylight, let alone on an eerie, dreary day, decided to read about such awful things? I was reading Poe for our English project on mysteries. But I wished I'd saved this part of my homework until my dad or Sharon had come home from work.

It's times like this — dark, stormy, lonely afternoons — when I miss Dawn more than ever. Dawn is one of my best friends and also my stepsister. She lives in California.

Who am I? I'm Mary Anne Spier, and I was wishing hard that I could put the sound of that beating heart out of my mind. It kept replaying like snatches of an irritating song stuck inside my brain. I turned on every light in the room, glad at least that I was nowhere near the secret passage that leads from our old farmhouse to the barn. It all sounds very mysterious, doesn't it?

I live in Stoneybrook, Connecticut, in a farmhouse built in 1795. If Edgar Allan Poe had ever visited Stoneybrook (and a professor from Stoneybrook University told our English class that he had) he would have been here when my house was still fairly new. I flipped to the part of my book that told a little about the author. Poe's stories were so sad and scary that I wondered if he'd been sad — or scary — himself. The short biography didn't mention Poe coming to Stoneybrook, but it did say that his mother and father had died when he was very young.

I could understand, better than most, why that would make a person sad. My mother died when I was a baby. However, unlike Poe, I still had my dad to take care of me. And now I also have a stepmother, Sharon, a stepsister, Dawn, and a stepbrother, Jeff. Sharon, Dad, and I live in Stoneybrook, but Dawn and Jeff live most of the year in California with their dad. How we became a family and moved into a farmhouse with a secret passage is a romantic story, not scary at all.

I met Dawn Schafer on her second day at Stoneybrook Middle School (SMS). We were both in seventh grade then. We're in eighth grade now. She was (and still is) tall, blonde, and very pretty. I was (and still am) short, with straight brown hair and brown eyes. I'm also very shy and wouldn't normally go out of my way to make a new friend. But I was in the middle of a fight with my regular friends, and Dawn showed up at the right time.

Dawn, her brother, and their mom had moved to Stoneybrook after Mr. and Mrs. Schafer divorced. For Sharon, Dawn's mom, this meant coming home since she'd grown up here. One day, when we were looking through some of Sharon's old yearbooks, we found out that she and my dad had dated each other. But then Sharon went out to California, met Mr. Schafer, and married him. And my dad stayed in Connecticut, became a lawyer, met my mom, and married her.

By the time Mrs. Schafer returned, both our parents were single again, so Dawn and I did a little matchmaking. Our parents ended up marrying one another after all.

Dawn is one of my two best friends. We have a lot in common, including the fact that we both love kids and baby-sitting. Most of my friends share these interests. We belong to a club called the Baby-sitters Club (more about that later), which Dawn also joined.

Jeff never felt at home here in Connecticut. Before long, he moved back to California to live with his dad. After awhile, Dawn moved back too. She just missed her dad and California too much. We talk on the phone as much as we can and write letters constantly, so we're almost as close as ever. Still, I wished she were in the house with me that afternoon.

Tigger, my gray-striped kitten, jumped on my lap and began to purr. I petted him. "You always know when I need a little company, don't you?" I said to him. He meowed, then curled up on my lap and fell asleep. I wasn't alone. Tigger was good company.

Before Dad married Sharon, he and I lived on Bradford Court, next door to Kristy Thomas (my other best friend) and across the street from another good friend, Claudia Kishi. Because I was so young when my mom died, I don't remember much about her. My dad says I look like her and act like her, though.

For a long time my dad was pretty strict, mostly because he wanted to prove he could be the best single parent ever. But that wasn't the only reason. My dad, who is an attorney, is very precise, and he likes rules. He used to have rules for lots of things — when and how long I could talk on the telephone, what kind of clothes I could wear, how I could style my hair. (I had to wear babyish jumpers and braid my hair every day.) I also had to be home earlier in the evening than almost anyone else in the seventh grade. I finally found the nerve to talk to my dad about it, and he let up a little. The first things to go were the hair and clothes rules. He didn't have to worry much because I didn't go crazy. I cut my hair and styled it in a way I like a lot. I dress the way some people describe as preppy, and I use a little makeup now too.

A lot of these changes happened before Dad and Sharon married, but Dad has loosened up even more since then. He had to. Sharon is very different from him! Combining our households took a little adjustment, especially at first.

Dad and I are organized with a capital O. Sharon isn't. For example, I opened the refrigerator for a snack after school today and found a stack of Sharon's papers on one of the shelves. When she opened her briefcase at work this morning, she probably found some celery or carrots. (I hope it wasn't a package of chicken.) Sharon and Dawn are the queens of health food, while Dad and I are big meat-and-potato eaters. Sharon has managed to ease us into healthier eating, but she hasn't convinced us to give up red meat.

I thought about drinking some juice, but if I stood up I'd have disturbed Tigger's nap. Still, maybe a drink would take my mind off the creepy sounds I'd heard, whether they were in my mind or for real. I still wasn't sure. The wind howled and groaned through the trees and around the corners of the house. I shivered a little.

Why hadn't I chosen an author other than Poe for my project? I had to admit he was an awfully good writer, since I couldn't stop thinking about the scenes he'd created. But the real reason I'd chosen Poe was silly. The morning the assignment was announced, Sharon had pointed out a business notice in the paper about a bookstore that would be opening in Stoneybrook. The name of the store was — ta-da! — Poe and Co. The article said that the store would specialize in mysteries. I love books and that means I love bookstores too, so this little piece of information stuck in my mind. When Edgar Allan Poe was listed as one of the authors we could choose to read, I felt it was fate. Now I was sitting alone in my house with a storm raging outside (not really raging, but it was raining pretty hard), thinking I could hear the tell-tale heart beating all around me.

I looked at the clock and saw that it was almost time to go to Claudia's house for our BSC meeting.

Slowly, I opened the Poe book again. It was a collection that combined a number of his short stories, including the first-ever detective stories ("The Murders in the Rue Morgue," "The Purloined Letter," and "The Gold-Bug"), with his poetry. Since I didn't have much time I turned to one of his poems, "Annabel Lee."

By the time I reached the end, my face was as wet as the ground outside. The poem wasn't so much scary as it was sad. I reached for a tissue and wiped away the tears. Not only did Annabel Lee's family break up her romance, but she died.

I keep a supply of tissues close at hand because I never know what's going to make me cry. It's not that I'm a baby or anything. I'm just very sensitive. I cry when I'm happy, when I'm sad, when I'm watching movies, when I'm reading books. Sometimes even TV commercials make me cry. The other day my boyfriend, Logan Bruno, compared the amount of rain we'd been having in Stoneybrook lately with my supply of tears. It had rained every day for almost three weeks and it seemed as if we would float away soon. Of course, Logan was teasing, and everything he says comes out in that sweet Southern accent of his, so I didn't mind at all.

Again, I turned to Poe's biography. His wife had died fairly young and he had had unhappy romances. As I read on I also found out that when he was alive, no one liked his work that much. Funny — today it seems as if everybody at least knows who he was. As Poe grew older, he became more and more despondent and even a little mad. He *was* a sad, sad man.

I gently picked up Tigger and placed him in the corner of the couch where I'd been sitting. I hated having to move him, but he didn't seem bothered. He gave a big sigh, wrapped his tail a little tighter around himself, and slept again.

There was more to our mystery unit than reading. I had to come up with a project using the work of the author I'd chosen in some way. I like to read and I like school. I even like projects. But I hadn't come up with a really good idea yet. I thought if I kept reading, something would come to me, but I didn't know how many more Poe stories I could read and still sleep at night.

What could I do? I could write a play based on one of his stories. But there was no way I could stand up in front of the class and perform it. I'm too shy for that.

I could write a report on Poe's life. Bo-o-o-ring!

I could buy a bird and teach it to say "Nevermore" like the raven in one of his poems.

I could try to write a story like one of Poe's, but I didn't think I could ever be as dark as he is. And, I'd probably scare myself silly if I tried to write one of his horror tales.

I like to quilt and I'd seen a picture of a cemetery quilt in a magazine once. I could make a quilt with "tombstones" for all the characters he killed in his stories. But that seemed too morbid.

If I walked slowly, I'd arrive at Claudia's house for the BSC meeting only a little bit early. My raincoat was still damp from walking home from school, but I put it on anyway. It was a yellow slicker with a navy blue lining. I love yellow and navy together. I picked up my umbrella on the way out the door and stepped into "Waterworld," as we'd started calling Stoneybrook.

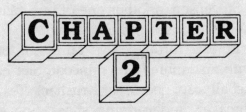

CHAPTER 2

Even with an umbrella and a raincoat, I felt the damp chill of the rain. It had been raining so long that water no longer soaked into the ground. It stood in puddles everyplace. There was no way to avoid walking through them.

Before Dad and I moved, I could run over to Claudia's house without an umbrella. Now I have a short hike to our BSC meetings. We meet every Monday, Wednesday, and Friday afternoon from five-thirty until six in Claudia's bedroom. Claud is the only one of us who has her own phone with her own number. That's important, because during our meeting times people call us to arrange for baby-sitters. Since there are a number of us in the BSC, we can always find them a reliable, experienced sitter.

I opened the front door to Claudia's house, shook the rain off my umbrella as best I could, and removed my raincoat. A little puddle formed at my feet as I decided what to do with my wet coat.

"Hold that door!" Kristy yelled from the street. Her brother Charlie drives Kristy and Abby Stevenson, another one of our members, to Claudia's house for the meetings.

Kristy ran through the rain, not bothering with an umbrella or raincoat. She had on a baseball cap, jeans, a Krushers T-shirt, a windbreaker, and running shoes. She leaped through the door, followed closely by Abby, who wore a green poncho over her jeans and shirt. When Abby threw back the hood of the poncho, I saw that the rain had made Abby's always curly hair even curlier.

"Thanks for keeping the door open for us," Kristy said, taking the stairs two at a time to the second floor of the Kishis' house.

"Yeah, thanks," echoed Abby, who was right on Kristy's heels.

I don't know which of them moves faster or more constantly. Each one would say that she was fastest.

I leaned my umbrella against the wall outside the door. Then I hung my raincoat on the coatrack in the hall, hoping it wouldn't drip too much. I followed Kristy and Abby to Claudia's room.

Kristy was already seated in Claudia's director's chair, the baseball cap replaced with a green visor and a pencil stuck over one ear.

"I don't know about the rest of you, but I'm so tired of rain. How much longer are we going to be able to keep afloat all the kids we baby-sit for?" Kristy said.

"Lately, when I'm baby-sitting, I feel like I'm sailing on a sinking ship," Abby said.

"It's sink or swim for the BSC," Claudia put in.

"Really, we need to come up with something. Every one of the kids I've baby-sat for this week is positively nutso, since they've been shut up inside for so long. Maybe we should talk about it under new business." Kristy is president of the BSC. She's the one who came up with the idea for the club, and she's the one who keeps coming up with plans for improving it. The idea for the BSC came about one afternoon as Kristy watched her mother call sitter after sitter, trying to find someone to watch David Michael, Kristy's younger brother. She thought how much easier it would be if there were one number parents could call to reach several sitters. Kristy's the type who doesn't just think up ideas, she puts them into play. The next thing we knew, we were part of the Baby-sitters Club.

Back then, Kristy and I still lived next door to each other on Bradford Court. Kristy lived with her mom; her two older brothers, Charlie and Sam; and David Michael. Her dad left the family when David Michael was a baby, and Kristy only hears from him once in awhile. Not long ago, Kristy's mom married a guy named Watson Brewer and the family moved to his mansion across town. Watson is a millionaire and their house is truly a mansion. In addition to Kristy and her brothers, Watson's two children from his first marriage, Karen and Andrew, live there every other month. And after Kristy's mom and Watson married, they adopted a little girl from Vietnam, Emily Michelle, who's now two and a half. When Emily Michelle came aboard, Kristy's grandmother moved in too, to help out. Since there are almost as many pets as people in the Thomas/Brewer household it's a good thing Kristy likes kids and animals as much as she does.

The BSC itself isn't the only good idea that Kristy has had. She also came up with the idea for Kid-Kits. Those are boxes — each of us has one — with books, toys, supplies, and activities inside. We take the Kid-Kits on baby-sitting jobs from time to time, for special occasions such as the arrival of a new baby, or to entertain a child who's been cooped up for awhile, and for rainy days. The Kid-Kits have been receiving quite a workout recently with all the rain. I had to agree with Kristy. It's been harder and harder to keep the kids I've been sitting for entertained. They're loaded with all kinds of stored-up energy from having to stay inside so much.

Kristy and I have been best friends as long as I can remember. We look a little bit alike, since we're both short (Kristy is the only person in eighth grade shorter than me) with brown hair and brown eyes, but we're very different in other ways. Kristy is a real take-charge (some would say bossy) person, and very athletic. Besides playing softball, she coaches a softball team made up of many of our baby-sitting charges. They're the Krushers featured on the shirt Kristy was wearing that day.

"Did you have softball practice today?" I asked.

Kristy rolled her eyes and shook her head. "I may have to turn the Krushers into a swim team if it doesn't stop raining." Knowing Kristy, she was as anxious to be outdoors and moving around as any of our charges.

"Who wants some chocolate?" Claudia asked, crawling out from under her bed, her hands filled with an assortment of miniature candy bars.

I held out my hand and she tossed a couple of the bite-size bars to me.

Claudia is vice-president of the Baby-sitters Club. As I mentioned, we use her room as our headquarters and it's her phone number that our clients call. She is also in charge of making sure none of us starves to death. Her endless supply of junk food allows her to achieve that goal. Notice how she had to crawl under the bed to find the snacks? That's because Claudia is addicted to junk food, and her parents don't approve. She has to hide it all over her room. They also don't think she should read so many Nancy Drew mysteries, which she loves almost as much as chocolate. So she hides those too.

Although Claudia is an eighth-grader like most of us BSC members, she recently spent some time back in seventh grade. But she caught up on the work and pulled up her grades, so she's been readmitted to eighth, which makes us happy. Claud isn't dumb or anything. She loves art, and it has always taken up a lot of her time and energy. If she'd concentrate on her other subjects the way she does on drawing and sculpting, she'd be near the top of our class. She loves anything to do with color, design, pictures, photography, paint, clay — you name it. One look at her and it's easy to see that she's talented. Claudia dresses like an artist (at least, the way I think an artist should dress), putting unique outfits together every day. She almost never wears the same thing twice. Today she had on a pair of jeans, but they weren't like anyone else's jeans. She'd painted raindrops down each leg. Over the jeans she wore a long white shirt and a gray vest. The vest had little umbrellas painted all over it. For earrings she was wearing paper parasols attached to gold chains.

People would look at Claudia even if she didn't dress the way she does. She's beautiful. Claudia is Japanese-American and has perfect skin, plus long, dark, shiny hair that she wears in tons of different styles. She lives with her mom, who is the head librarian at the Stoneybrook Public Library; her dad, who works for an investment firm in Stamford; and her older sister, Janine. Janine is so-o-o smart. She's a junior at Stoneybrook High School, but she also takes classes at Stoneybrook University — for fun. Claudia's grandmother Mimi lived with them until she died not long ago. Claudia misses her a lot, which I completely understand. Mimi was very special to me too.

"Maybe we could practice in the gym some afternoon," Abby said to Kristy. "We're starting the softball season late this year."

"The only good thing is that none of the other teams can practice either," Kristy reminded her.

"Aren't you anxious to begin?" asked Abby.

"Of course, but I can't stop the rain," said Kristy.

17

Abby Stevenson is the newest member of the BSC and our alternate officer. That means she fills in for any officer who's absent. She recently moved to Stoneybrook from Long Island, with her mother and her sister, Anna — her identical twin. We asked both Anna and Abby to join the BSC, but Anna decided she was too busy with her music. She's a talented violinist and wants to be a professional musician. She practices a lot.

Abby, on the other hand, is an athlete. When she isn't practicing for some team sport, she often runs from her house to Claudia's for our meetings. (Abby lives a couple of houses down from Kristy, so it's a good, long run.) Even now she was moving from one place in Claudia's room to another, not sitting still for more than a minute at a time. She's an assistant coach for Kristy's Krushers, and she also plays on a soccer team.

Abby's dad died in a car accident when she was nine years old, and although she seldom talks about it, I don't think she's quite over it yet. Her mom works as an executive editor for a publishing company in New York City. Abby and Anna recently celebrated their Bat Mitzvah, a ceremony for Jewish girls turning thirteen.

One thing that always surprises me about Abby is that although she's allergic to tons of things, she doesn't let that stop her from doing whatever she wants to do. She has asthma too, and sometimes has to use an inhaler to help her breathe. She also has a terrific sense of humor about her allergies and everything else.

"Has anybody else thought that it's almost time to start building an ark?" Abby asked, making us all laugh.

"What's so funny?" Stacey McGill asked as she took off her rain hat — not one of those dorky clear plastic ones, but a wide-brimmed navy hat that looked great on her — and shook out her blonde hair.

Stacey *would* wear a long navy coat while the rest of us wear slickers or ponchos or, like Kristy, nothing to keep the rain off. Stacey moved to Stoneybrook from New York City the summer before seventh grade, when her dad was transferred here. Mr. McGill was later transferred back to New York City, and the family moved with him again. We missed Stacey a lot. We were glad when she moved back not long afterward, although the circumstances weren't the happiest — her mom and dad were divorcing. Stacey and Mrs. McGill returned to Stoneybrook, but her dad stayed in an apartment in the city. Stacey visits him when she can. She's a bit more sophisticated than the rest of us, probably because of all the time she's spent in New York City, and it especially shows in the way she dresses. Her clothes are extremely trendy and she spends as much time putting together outfits as Claudia does, although their styles are different. Today she'd painted her nails navy blue to match her outfit. She wore a navy blue miniskirt and a white ribbed turtleneck with matching white ribbed stockings. Although it sounds plain, nothing looks plain on Stacey. Around her neck she wore a thick gold chain that hung about halfway down her sweater.

Stacey is tall and thin. She has big blue eyes with dark lashes that make them look even bluer. She's done some modeling from time to time.

Because she's so good at math, Stacey is the treasurer of the BSC. Every week she collects dues from each of us. Then it's her job to keep track of how much money we spend and for what. We use the money to help pay Claudia's phone bill, to pay Charlie for driving Kristy and Abby to our meetings, and to pay for materials to replenish the Kid-Kits. If anything is left over, it goes for pizza or some other treat.

Stacey plopped down on the bed between me and Claudia. Claudia opened a drawer in her desk and pulled out some popcorn. "I hope it's not stale," she said.

There's another reason Stacey seems more mature than the rest of us. She has diabetes.

That means her body has trouble processing sugar. She's very careful about what she eats (no sweets, for example), and she has to give herself insulin injections every day. Stacey will always have diabetes, but as long as she pays attention to her diet, monitors her blood sugar, and takes her insulin, she should be okay. Claudia keeps a stash of healthy snacks for Stacey in addition to the junk food she serves the rest of us.

Mallory Pike and Jessica Ramsey were the last to arrive. I noticed that Kristy looked at the clock as they came into the room. Kristy is very strict about starting meetings on time, and it was almost five-thirty.

Jessi and Mal are our junior officers. They're in sixth grade at SMS. As junior officers, they only baby-sit in the afternoons unless it's for their own families.

Jessi loves ballet. She often wears her dark hair in a bun, which shows off her big dark eyes and smooth, cocoa-colored skin. She's very slender, and she moves so gracefully. In addition to dancing, Jessi loves books, horses, and of course, baby-sitting. She has a younger sister, Becca, and a baby brother, Squirt (officially John Philip, Jr.). Since Jessi's parents work, her aunt Cecelia lives with the family and helps take care of the kids.

Jessi and Mal met almost as soon as Jessi

moved to Stoneybrook from New Jersey. They were in the same homeroom, and they quickly became best friends.

Mal also loves books and horses. As you might imagine, she and Jessi like books about horses best of all. Someday, Mal would like to write and illustrate children's books. She should have plenty of stories to tell, since she has seven younger brothers and sisters. After Mal came the triplets, Adam, Byron, and Jordan; then Vanessa; Nicky; Margo; and Claire. The BSC gets plenty of business just sitting for the Pike family. Mal has curly reddish-brown hair and blue eyes. She wears braces and glasses, and she thinks this moves her out of the "cute" category, but she's very wrong.

The phone started ringing almost as soon as Kristy called the meeting to order, on the dot of five-thirty, so I had to open the record book right away. One of my jobs as club secretary is to keep up the club record book. I'm very proud of the fact that I've never made a mistake in it. We keep the names, addresses, phone numbers, pay rate, and any special information about the children we sit for, as well as our schedules, in the record book.

The way the club works is that whoever is closest to the phone answers it, takes the information about the job (who, when, where, how many children), then tells the caller that we'll phone back as soon as a sitter is assigned. I check the schedule to see who is available, then we let the client know who will be sitting.

The calls kept coming. I was starting to think that a lot of parents were as tired of staying out of the rain as we — and the kids — were.

Another of Kristy's great ideas is our club notebook. We write up each of our jobs in the notebook, and then everybody reads the entries once a week. It's a good way to keep track of what's going on with our sitting charges. Some of us like to write in the notebook more than others. Mallory and Kristy love it; Claudia hates it. It's definitely a lot more fun to read what everybody else has written than it is to write in it.

Today no one had time to read or write. We were too busy scheduling sitting jobs.

"There's nobody who can take the job on Sunday afternoon," I said after checking and rechecking the schedules. "We're going to have to call Logan or Shannon."

Logan Bruno, who, as I've already mentioned, is my boyfriend, is also an associate member of the BSC. We call on our associates when we have jobs the regular members can't fill. Logan moved to Stoneybrook from Louisville, Kentucky, where he had done some baby-sitting. I noticed him the very first day he showed up at our school. At first I thought he

23

was Cam Geary, my favorite TV star. Believe me, Logan is as cute as Cam. He has great blue eyes and blondish-brown hair that curls (although I think he wishes it wouldn't). He's as good a baby-sitter as any of the regular members of the club, but he tried coming to our meetings and didn't feel very comfortable.

Shannon Kilbourne is our other associate member. She's the only one of us who doesn't go to SMS. She goes to Stoneybrook Day School, a private school. Shannon is in the eighth grade and lives on Kristy and Abby's street. At first, Kristy thought Shannon was stuck-up, but as we got to know her better, we found out she's a lot of fun. She has two younger sisters and a dog, Astrid of Grenville, who is the mother of Kristy's puppy, Shannon. Shannon is involved in lots of activities at Stoneybrook Day — plays, Honor Society, tutoring, Astronomy Club, debate, and a few other things. Part of the reason she's an associate BSC member is she doesn't have time to do everything!

That leaves only one other member of the BSC, my stepsister, Dawn Schafer. Before she moved back to California, Dawn was our alternate officer. Now she's an honorary BSC member and takes part in our activities when she's here.

I called Logan, and he agreed to take the

Sunday job. As soon as I hung up the telephone, it rang again. Since I was closest, I answered. I heard a man on the other end of the phone clear his throat. I waited for him to speak.

"My name is Mr. Cates, and one of the men who's been working for me gave me your number," he said. "We've moved into town recently and I have two children, a boy and a girl, and I could use some assistance."

"You mean, you need a baby-sitter?" I asked.

"Yes, that's right. See, I'm opening a bookstore. . . ." (My heart did a little flip-flop. As I mentioned, I love bookstores.) "It's a mystery bookstore, called Poe and Co."

The flip-flop turned into a drumming that reminded me of "The Tell-Tale Heart" again. Was this another stroke of fate? I hoped he needed a sitter at a time I was available, although I knew I had to offer the job to everyone.

"The store will be in the Benson Dalton Gable house. We have an apartment upstairs. Is there anybody located out this way who could sit for the kids?" Mr. Cates finished.

"When do you need a sitter?" I asked as coolly as I could. I wondered if he heard my tell-tale heart.

"Thursday, tomorrow. Tomorrow afternoon would be great, around four. I'm trying to prepare the store to open as soon as possible. Tom

25

and Gillian, the kids, are tired of the rain, tired of unpacking books, tired of living in a half-finished house . . . tired of me, to be quite honest. I thought if we could give them a change of pace it would help."

Tomorrow. I was available tomorrow. "May I have your telephone number, please? We'll check our schedules and call you right back to tell you who will be your sitter," I said. I wrote his number on a scrap of paper. "And," I added, "how old are," I looked at the names I'd scribbled down, "Tom and Gillian?"

"They're, let's see, Tom is ten and Gillian is seven."

"Thanks. We'll call you right back."

"That's a new client," I announced as I hung up the phone. "His name is Mr. Cates and he's opening a bookstore here."

Mal sat up a little straighter. "A bookstore?"

I nodded. "A mystery bookstore named Poe and Co."

"I think my mom mentioned that," said Mal.

"He needs a sitter tomorrow afternoon." I pretended to study the schedule. "Kristy, you and I are both free."

"A bookstore. That sounds pretty exciting," said Kristy.

I looked up at her. A sporting goods store was more to her liking. She was grinning at me.

"I've had a lot of jobs this week. Go ahead if you want it," Kristy said.

I grabbed the phone and punched in the number, quickly, as if Kristy might change her mind. "Mr. Cates?" I said when he answered. "It's me, Mary Anne Spier from the Baby-sitters Club. I'd be glad to sit for your children tomorrow afternoon." I listened to him for a minute.

"I'll walk over," I continued. "I'm looking forward to meeting Tom and Gillian." The job seemed meant for me. I was working on a mystery project and Edgar Allan Poe was my subject. Poe and Co. was the name of the book-store and it specialized in mysteries. Maybe spending time at a place named after my sub-ject would spark a unique idea for my project. I couldn't wait.

I turned back to the conversation the rest of the club was having.

"Nobody has even one idea about what we could do to keep the kids entertained in spite of the rain?" Kristy asked.

"If I had one, I'd throw it out to see if it would float," Jessi assured Kristy.

Everybody groaned. Jokes about the rain were old, old, old.

CHAPTER 3

It was still raining when I walked to Poe and Co. on Thursday afternoon. I slowed as I approached the place. The Benson Dalton Gable house had been empty for almost as long as I could remember. Each year it looked a little shabbier and seemed to sink a little lower, but Mr. Cates had been very busy and the house was looking quite prim now. It was two stories high, and quite wide. The roof sat on top like a little flat hat with lots of scalloped shingles. The windows were high and narrow, with no curtains. They reminded me of something I'd read in another Edgar Allan Poe story, "The Fall of the House of Usher." They were "vacant eye-like windows" like the windows in the story. As the narrator approaches the house, it is a stormy day, with clouds swirling in the sky. I remembered that the man had said something about being caught up in the owner's wild superstitions. I swallowed hard. I wouldn't let that happen to me. After all, it was a house — a kind of scary-looking house, but just a house. I would be able to handle this.

Before I knocked on the door, it flew open and a man started backing toward me, carrying some long boards. I quickly moved out of the way, but the front porch was small and I had to press against the porch railings.

"Sorry," the man said gruffly. "Didn't know anybody was out here. Place isn't open yet."

"I'm the baby-sitter," I said.

"Good luck," the man said. "Cates is inside." He turned and walked toward a pickup truck parked in the mud nearby.

I stepped inside and looked around. I could hear hammers pounding steadily. Bookshelves were standing all over the room in no apparent order, and boxes were stacked everywhere. Facing the door was a high black counter. A blonde head popped up from behind the counter, and a woman smiled at me, flashing a set of dimples.

"Hi, I'm Mary Anne Spier. I'm here to baby-sit for Tom and Gillian," I said.

"Larry! The baby-sitter is here," the woman called toward the back of the house.

She turned back to me. "I'm Cillia Spark. I'm helping Larry set up the bookstore. And it will be a bookstore very soon."

A tall man, with dark hair long enough to

29

hang over his collar in the back, joined us. "Tom! Gillian!" he called. "Hi, baby-sitter. We're glad to see you. I'm Larry Cates and this is —"

"I've already introduced myself," said Ms. Spark, showing her dimples again.

"The house, I mean the store, looks really good from the outside," I said.

"We've fixed it up a little," said Mr. Cates. "We still have plenty to do, as you can see." He pointed at the shelves and boxes surrounding us.

"Here, let me take your coat. I better hang it in the closet or it'll be covered with dust before you leave," said Ms. Spark. "Larry, have you seen my sketches for the shelf placement in here? I thought I left them on the counter, but I can't find them now. The guys are ready to start lining up the shelves."

"I haven't seen them," said Mr. Cates with a shrug. "We can ask the kids."

Two children appeared in the doorway to the hall. I could see steps rising behind them leading up to the second floor. The boy was tall and thin with dark wavy hair like his dad's. He had dark eyes surrounded by dark lashes. The girl was short and also thin. She had the same dark eyes as her brother, but her hair was lighter brown, very long and very straight, with bangs. It needed a good brushing. I could see tangles from where I stood.

30

"Tom, Gillian, this is Mary Anne. She's in a club that sends out baby-sitters to all the kids in Stoneybrook," said Mr. Cates.

I started to correct him and say not to *all* the kids, but I decided I better concentrate on these two kids. "Hi, Tom, hi, Gillian. It's nice to meet you. Have you started school yet?"

They didn't answer.

"They're going to Stoneybrook Elementary," said Mr. Cates.

"Has either of you seen my sketches for where the bookshelves go?" Ms. Spark asked them.

The kids turned to her, frowning. Tom crossed his arms over his chest and shook his head. Gillian looked up at Tom, then did the same thing.

"If you do see them, will you bring them down? Please?" Ms. Spark smiled brightly at them.

"Maybe you two could show me around a little bit, tell me what the store's going to look like," I suggested.

"Good idea," said Mr. Cates, sounding relieved. "You can start with Benson Dalton Gable's office. I haven't changed it that much. It's the one thing I plan to leave the way it was."

"You guys will have to tell me about Benson Dalton Gable," I said as I joined the kids in the hall.

"He was a mystery writer, a contemporary of Poe's," Ms. Spark said, not giving the children a chance to tell me anything. "He lived here all his life. Larry bought the house from his descendants. But you've probably never heard of any of Gable's work. That's why Larry named the store Poe and Co. and not Gable and Co." She and Mr. Cates laughed.

"And there's lots of speculation that Poe visited Gable here. Just think. Edgar Allan Poe walked on the same floor you're walking on now," Mr. Cates said, a touch of awe in his voice.

I looked down at the floor, then at Tom and Gillian. They rolled their eyes.

"The floors are all new," Tom said. "The place was a wreck, and it isn't much better now. We had a nice house before." He turned and walked toward the back of the house. Gillian glanced at me to see if I was coming too, then followed her brother.

"Here's the office where the old guy wrote stuff." Tom flung open a door, then leaned against the wall outside the room.

I peeked inside. There was a huge desk in the middle of the room and shelves along one wall. Two windows overlooked the backyard.

"That's going to be a parking lot," said Gillian. "We won't have any grass here."

Tom walked away. "Here's the kitchen, but

we never cook anything. My mom used to cook the best spaghetti. . . ." He sighed.

Where was Mrs. Cates? I wondered. This was the first time she'd been mentioned, and there didn't seem to be any sign of her. I knew better than to ask about her, though. The kids would talk about her when they were ready.

"This is the downstairs bathroom," said Gillian, continuing the tour, "but anybody who comes in the store can use it anytime they want. It's not private."

"And that's Dad's office." Tom pointed to a closed door. "That room, with a table and carts in it, is where all the books come in. The rest of the downstairs is going to be the store. There's a basement, and we live upstairs."

"How do you like Stoneybrook so far?" I asked.

"Hate it," Tom mumbled.

Gillian nodded. "It's rained every day since we moved here. I've only played outside on the school playground two times."

"It can't rain forever," I said. "When it stops you'll see that there's lots to do here. But we don't have to wait for it to stop raining. Want to play some games? Do you have any board games?"

"Packed," said Tom.

"Packed," repeated Gillian.

"Want to play store?" I grinned.

"We lived right down the street from a video arcade at our old house," said Tom. "And Mom took us there whenever we wanted, didn't she, Gillian?"

Gillian looked at Tom, a puzzled expression on her face, then nodded.

"I'm afraid there aren't any video arcades nearby," I said, wishing I'd brought my Kid-Kit. "You guys must like books. And your dad owns a bookstore."

"You want to read us a story?" asked Tom.

"We could read —" Gillian said.

"No way," her brother cut in.

"What *would* you like to do?" I asked, trying another tack.

"Move out of this place," said Tom.

"How's it going?" Mr. Cates asked, sticking his head around the corner.

I made myself smile. "Fine," I answered.

"If you kids are looking for something to do, why don't you go upstairs and unpack some of the boxes in your rooms? You might find something you haven't played with for awhile. You wouldn't mind supervising, would you, Mary Anne? We haven't had a lot of time to spend on organizing the house."

"I wouldn't mind at all," I said, actually feeling grateful that there was something to do.

"Come on, Gillian," said Tom as he stomped up the stairs.

Again, Gillian waited for me before following Tom. "My room is up here," she said. "It has roses on the wallpaper."

"That sounds very pretty," I replied.

"And my room has guns," said Tom.

"Dad's going to change it first chance he has," Gillian whispered to me. "He doesn't like guns that much."

I heard the outside door open again.

"Mail's here," Mr. Cates said, then I heard something smack against the counter.

"Mail," said Gillian to Tom.

They thundered down the stairs, pushed past me, and hurried into the main room of the store.

Tom grabbed the stack of mail and shuffled through it. When he reached the last letter, he threw it down. The mail slid all over the counter, some of it falling to the floor. "Nothing," he said to his little sister.

I saw tears brighten Gillian's eyes. She took a deep breath that sounded almost like a sob.

Mr. Cates had watched the kids as they looked through the mail. He looked as though he wished he'd never announced it was there. He knelt between Tom and Gillian. "Mom is busy settling into her new place too. She has a new job and a new apartment. She's probably waiting to write a really long letter to tell you all about it. Maybe tomorrow."

"That's what you said yesterday," said Tom.

"She'll write," Mr. Cates said. "Go on upstairs. The one who unpacks the most boxes chooses where we eat tonight. Deal?"

"Deal," said Gillian softly. I almost didn't hear her.

Tom turned and climbed the stairs slowly.

"Mary Anne?" Mr. Cates said.

I'd started to follow the kids, but he motioned to me.

"The kids' mom, my wife, left not long ago and the kids still aren't used to it yet. They may seem a little difficult, but keep in mind we're all trying to make a new start and it's hard for them," he said.

"I understand. It's okay. I've had to deal with some pretty big changes too."

"Thanks," Mr. Cates added.

I smiled at him. I was glad for the information. It explained a couple of things.

Before I even entered Tom's room, I heard him grumbling.

"Books. Bookstores," he muttered.

"What about books and bookstores?" I asked, coming into his room. On the bed a sleeping bag was spread over the mattress — no sheets or blankets. A suitcase with clothes spilling out sat in the middle of the floor. Boxes were everywhere. The room was a disaster.

"Dad and his books. He had to open a bookstore no matter what. Mom didn't want to at all. That's probably why she left," said Tom.

"There are probably lots of reasons," I said cautiously. I knew enough about life to realize that big changes, such as a parent leaving the family, seldom happened because of one thing. Or one person.

"You don't know anything," said Tom.

"You're right. I don't. Maybe you should talk to your dad."

Tom pulled open a box and dumped the contents on the floor. I saw albums of baseball cards, a baseball glove, and some pictures.

"Where are you going to put all that?" I asked.

"I'll find a place." He opened one of the albums and started looking through it.

"You want to make up the bed? If you tell me where the sheets are, I'll help you," I suggested.

"Maybe later."

"It might not hurt to unpack your clothes," I tried again.

"Uh-huh. Shouldn't you go check on Gillian?"

"Okay. I'll be back in a little while." I walked down the hall to Gillian's room.

"This *is* pretty wallpaper," I said, admiring the pink roses.

Gillian smiled. "My bedspread from my old house looks good with it, doesn't it?"

The bedspread was also pink, with ruffles. It reminded me of the way my room used to look before Dad let me redecorate. "It does look good." Gillian's bed had sheets on it and I could see that she'd already unpacked some of her clothes. They hung neatly in the closet. She was unpacking books now, and putting them on a shelf over her desk.

"How many boxes has Tom unpacked?" she asked.

"He's working on his first one."

"Tom doesn't listen very well," Gillian confided in a low voice. "Sometimes Mom would have to tell him a million times to make his bed and clean up his room or bring his dirty clothes down to the laundry room. She used to get really tired of it. But I didn't keep my room very neat then either. I do now, though, don't I?"

"It's great," I assured her.

"I wish Mom could see how much better I am. I could be a big help now."

My heart was breaking. Gillian thought her mom had left because of them. Tom, on the other hand, seemed to think it was because of their dad. Who knew?

"Gillian, you were probably a big help to your mom all along. It wasn't your fault she left," I said. "Have you talked to your dad about this?"

Gillian shook her head. "He doesn't like to talk about Mom much. I think he misses her too. At least he did before Ms. Spark came. Do you think they're boyfriend and girlfriend? Tom said he thinks so."

Whoa! Another news flash. I had seen a little of that when Ms. Spark smiled at Mr. Cates earlier.

"Did I hear my name?" Ms. Spark stepped into the room. "How many boxes have you unpacked, Gillian? I want you to win because I know you'll choose pizza and your dad invited me to stay for supper." She smoothed Gillian's hair.

Gillian jerked away from her, squatting down to take another armload of books out of the box.

I looked around and found a brush, comb, and mirror lined up perfectly on the dresser. "I'll brush those tangles out of your hair for you if you want," I said to Gillian.

She finished putting the books away, then sat in front of me on the floor. "When I play at school and don't have it pulled back in a ponytail, the tangles get worse," Gillian said. "I can't comb them out as well as Mom did. You won't pull, will you? *She* pulls." She looked at Ms. Spark, then down at the floor.

"I admit I need a little practice," said Ms. Spark. "I haven't had long hair for awhile now. And mine never looked as good as yours anyway. It's too curly to wear long." Ms. Spark ran her fingers through her hair, smiling.

Carefully, I combed out Gillian's tangles.

"Do you mind if I look around for my sketches in here?" Ms. Spark asked. "I doubt they're here, but I can't find them anyplace else."

"They aren't here," said Gillian.

"They aren't in Tom's room either," said Ms. Spark. "I guess I'll look in the den and in your dad's room."

"Did you check in the hall closet?" I looked up at the sound of Tom's voice. He was lounging in the doorway, watching us.

"Not yet, but I will." Ms. Spark had to squeeze through the door. Tom didn't move even the slightest bit.

"Let Ms. Spark through please, Tom," I said. He turned sideways so she could pass a little easier.

Tom watched Ms. Spark. I heard the door open, then a sharp scream. Gillian shot up off the floor. I ran after them to see what had happened.

"Pluto, you rascal!" I heard Ms. Spark say.

"What's going on up here?" Mr. Cates joined us in the hall.

A black cat faced Ms. Spark, its back arched and tail puffed. Pluto definitely did not look happy.

"Pluto was in the closet, and when I opened the door he jumped onto me. I thought I was going to have a heart attack," Ms. Spark explained.

"At least you didn't find a body in there," said Mr. Cates. He and Ms. Spark laughed. "I named this cat Pluto after the black cat in the Poe story called 'The Black Cat.' It's the one in which the man kills his wife and bricks her up in the basement, and the cat is in there too. When the police come, the cat alerts them to the body by meowing behind the wall. It's a good story. And every bookstore needs a cat. For Poe and Co., a black cat was the obvious choice and Pluto the obvious name."

I guessed I'd have to read "The Black Cat" now.

I watched as Tom nudged Gillian. They were trying not to laugh. I had a notion that Pluto didn't end up in that closet by accident. It grew stronger when I remembered that Tom had suggested Ms. Spark look for the plans in the closet.

"Come see what I did today, Daddy," Gillian said, tugging on his hand.

"This almost looks like a place to live in instead of a storehouse," Mr. Cates said, peering into Gillian's room.

"I unpacked more boxes than you did," said Tom, counting the empty cardboard boxes stacked against Gillian's wall. "I did four."

That surprised me. When I'd left the room, he hadn't unpacked one.

I was even more surprised when I stepped inside his room. The bed was made — with sheets. Clothes hung in the closet, and four empty boxes were on the floor.

"Did you put stuff away or dump it in the drawers?" Mr. Cates asked.

"I put it away in the drawers," Tom said.

Gillian gave her brother a look. I've seen similar looks pass between Dawn and Jeff. I think it's a brother/sister thing.

"And I want Chinese food," he added.

"Cillia doesn't like it," said Mr. Cates.

"You said the one who unpacked the most boxes could choose," said Tom.

This time Gillian smiled at her brother.

"I'll grab a hamburger when we go out to pick up the food," Ms. Spark said.

"I want to eat in a restaurant," said Tom. His tone bordered on whiny.

"We'll see," said Mr. Cates. "Mary Anne, I want to thank you for all you've done. I wish I had ten of you to help me get the rest of this place in shape. Will you be available to sit another time?"

I started hearing heartbeats again. I hadn't spent much time in the bookstore, and I was dying to see what books were packed inside the boxes. Was Mr. Cates going to carry children's books?

"I can't promise you ten, but I'd like to come back, and some of the others in the BSC might want to help out if you think you can use us," I said.

"Use you? We'd love the help. The pay won't be very much, but I could find something. If we don't open soon, the bill collectors are going to outnumber the customers," said Mr. Cates. "I could use as many of you from the BSC as you can send."

"I'll see what I can do," I promised. I knew Mal would want to come, and Jessi. In fact, I couldn't think of anyone who wouldn't want to come. Anybody who didn't want to work with the books could help out with Tom and Gillian.

"We're about ready to finish up for the day. The workmen have all left," said Mr. Cates.

I noticed, once he mentioned it, that the hammering had stopped.

We trooped down the steps to the main room. I couldn't see much difference from when I'd gone upstairs.

"We have to find my sketches before we

can put the shelves in," Ms. Spark explained. "They fit in a certain way."

"Is this what you're looking for?" Tom pulled a stack of oversized paper off a shelf behind the counter.

"My sketches!" Ms. Spark laid them out on the counter. "They were on the shelf? I can't believe it. It's like 'The Purloined Letter,' when the thief hides the stolen letter in plain sight and no one can find it. I can't believe I didn't see them!"

"We need a Dupin around here," said Mr. Cates, as the two of them laughed together — again. Maybe Tom was right. They might not be boyfriend and girlfriend yet, but something was there.

I recognized that name, Dupin, and the story about the letter. Dupin was the detective Poe wrote about in several stories. Mr. Cates and Ms. Spark knew an awful lot about Edgar Allan Poe. And, they had a lot of fun using what they knew.

I turned to Tom and Gillian to say good-bye. They were glaring at Ms. Spark. Exactly how did her sketches find their way to that shelf? I wondered. I decided I'd better warn the rest of the BSC that Tom and Gillian like to "tease" Ms. Spark.

CHAPTER 4

Saturday dawned dull and rainy again. Mr. Cates had called us at the BSC meeting the afternoon before and asked whether some of us could help out at the store. He also asked if someone could baby-sit for Tom and Gillian on Saturday and suggested that they might like to go to the movies for a change of scene. Claudia had agreed to baby-sit for the kids. As I'd predicted, Mal volunteered immediately to help out in the store. I wanted to help too. Kristy and Logan ended up going with us as well.

Since the last time I'd been at Poe and Co., someone had laid boards on top of bricks so we could approach the door without losing our shoes in the mud. There were three umbrellas on the front porch when we arrived. Mine joined them. Kristy and Logan wore hooded jackets instead of carrying umbrellas.

A boy who looked old enough for high school was standing behind the counter, his chin resting in his hands, when we walked inside. A lone hammer pounded somewhere in the house.

"Store's not open," the boy said, his hands pressing against his chin. This kept his jaw from moving and gave his words an odd sound.

"We're here to help Mr. Cates," I replied. "Is he around?"

"He's talking to my dad in the office." This time he stood up a little straighter. "What are you helping him do?"

"Fix up the bookstore so that it's ready to open," I said.

I was glad to see Ms. Spark come into the room. "Mary Anne! It's so good to see you again," she said. She carried rolled-up sketches under her arm. I guess she wasn't letting them out of her sight again. I didn't blame her.

"Are you ready to work?" Ms. Spark asked.

"We are," I answered. "This is Kristy Thomas, Mallory Pike, and Logan Bruno. They're members of the BSC too."

"Oh." The boy snorted and shook his head.

I ignored him and continued with the introductions. "This is Ms. Spark. She's helping Mr. Cates set up the store."

"So glad that all of you could come," Ms. Spark said, showing her dimples. She smiled so much that they seldom disappeared. "I bet it looks as if I'm not working very hard. But you should have seen the place when we started. What a mess!"

"Hey, you're talking about my property," the boy said.

When Ms. Spark looked at him her smile dimmed a little. "This is Alex Gable. Larry — Mr. Cates — bought the house from Alex's father."

"We are the only living descendants of Benson Dalton Gable," Alex announced. "He was a famous mystery writer in his day, far more popular than Edgar Allan Poe."

"I don't know if I'd go that far," said Ms. Spark.

"In Poe and Gable's day, literature was appreciated much more than schlock," said Alex.

"I wouldn't say that Poe wrote schlock. His work has endured across generations. He wrote some of the best-known works in American literary history," said Ms. Spark.

Kristy and Logan wandered off and started looking around the room as Ms. Spark and Alex argued over the merits of Poe versus Gable. Mal and I stayed to listen. I still had to come up with a topic for my project, after all.

Alex shrugged. "If we could find all of Gable's works, he might become more well-known than Poe."

"Perhaps," said Ms. Spark.

Alex had made one point that I knew was valid. I'd read that in Poe's day, people didn't like the stories and poems he wrote nearly as much as they do now. I'd known the name Gable because everyone in Stoneybrook called the house "the Gable place," but I hadn't known that Gable wrote mysteries like Poe did. Alex knew a lot, but I could tell from the way he glanced at us as he spoke that he was trying to impress Ms. Spark and us.

Maybe I could use Gable in my mystery project. "Is there a book of Gable's stories?" I asked.

"No. At least, not yet," said Alex. "My dad and I have all his papers — the ones that we've been able to find so far. All his stories were published in magazines." He looked around the room. "And we plan to publish them in a book someday. Then we'll see who is more popular."

"I'm sure Mr. Cates will be the first to stock an anthology of Benson Dalton Gable mysteries," Ms. Spark said to Alex before she turned to us. "You're probably anxious to start work. I'm sure you didn't come here to listen to a debate about literature. There are several things that need to be done. I need someone to check in books. We don't have the computer system completely up and running yet, though I'm hopeful that the electricians will finish the wiring today and we can go on-line soon. Still, Larry wants to know if we're receiving all the books he ordered, and the only way to do that is to check against the invoices."

"I'll do that," Mal said.

"It will probably take two people. Larry has a room in the back that's set up for receiving books. There's a big table you can spread them out on. After the books are checked in, you can transfer them to carts."

"I'll help Mal," Kristy offered.

"Great. Mary Anne, Logan, do you like to paint?"

"That sounds good," said Logan.

I nodded.

"Okay, see the new drywall along that side of the room?" She pointed to a wall that had been replaced. The gray of the drywall (or what I guessed was drywall) was marked with white lines and spots. "We need to paint over it with a coat of primer to ready it for the final paint job. Then we're going to cover it up with shelves, of course, but that's the way it goes.

"Let's find you some old shirts to protect your clothes, then fix you up with brushes." She handed us shirts already spotted with paint. I slipped mine on and rolled up the sleeves. Next, she gave us paintbrushes and primer.

Logan and I studied the wall we were to

"prime." A brick fireplace with a carved mantel was in the middle of the wall. It was a nice touch for the store, but I sure didn't want to drip paint on it.

"I'll show Mal and Kristy what to do, then I'll come back and see if you need anything else," said Ms. Spark.

"Do you have some plastic we could spread over the fireplace and on the floor?" Logan asked.

"Of course! I forgot. It's in the back room. I'll show you where."

"I could go with you and bring it back," said Alex. "I'm not doing anything anyway."

"Thanks, that would help," said Ms. Spark.

"That fireplace and mantel are original to the house. I'd hate to see them spotted with paint," Alex added.

Logan and I exchanged looks. Logan opened a gallon container of the primer and stirred it with a long wooden paddle.

"I'll find the plastic," I finally said when Alex didn't return.

The door to Mr. Cates's office was open a crack. I could hear his voice and that of another man talking and laughing. Continuing down the hall, I glanced into the room Benson Dalton Gable had once used as an office, then across the hall into the long, narrow room where Ms.

Spark was giving Mal and Kristy instructions on how to check in books.

"Did you give Alex the plastic?" I asked.

"I told him where to find it," said Ms. Spark, a frown flickering across her face. "Didn't he bring it to you?"

"No, not yet."

"It's on the porch off the kitchen. We've been using that area to store some of the supplies."

"Thanks. I'll find it." I stepped into the kitchen from the hallway, and Alex entered from the basement at the same moment. I stopped abruptly and the surprise I felt at seeing him there instead of on the porch — and without the plastic — must have shown on my face. He immediately began to explain.

"I love this house," Alex said. "I've spent a lot of time here. The guys working in the basement are guys I know, and I wanted to say hi." He stuck his head inside a portion of the kitchen wall that had been torn away but was not finished yet. Electrical wires were sticking out of the opening.

"What are you looking for?" I asked.

He started and turned quickly. "Interesting to see what's at the heart of an old house, isn't it?"

I shrugged. I didn't know many high school

boys who cared as much about old houses and literature as Alex. And, all of a sudden, he'd decided to be friendly. Earlier, he had barely noticed us.

"This is a sound building, even if it has run down some in the past few years," said Alex. "As the saying goes, they don't build 'em like this anymore."

"I guess not." I opened the door to the back porch.

"Let me help you carry that to the front," Alex offered.

"Thanks," I said. We gathered armfuls of plastic sheeting and carried it to the front of the store.

Alex draped a piece over the fireplace, covering both mantel and hearth. Logan and I spread the remaining sheets over the floor. I felt a lot better about painting now.

"Have you been upstairs since they've redone it?" Alex asked me.

"I was helping Tom and Gillian, Mr. Cates's children, unpack the last time I was here," I said.

"I sure would like to see what Mr. Cates has done up there. Do you think he'd mind?"

"Ask him," I answered.

The front door opened and wind swept through, bringing dampness with it and ruffling the plastic we'd spread on the floor. We scrambled to keep it in place.

"Hello," a woman's voice greeted us.

The voice sounded slightly familiar, but I couldn't place it. I looked up and saw the professor from Stoneybrook University who had visited our English class.

"Ramona Kingsolver," she said in her hurried voice. "For Mr. Cates." Just as on the day she'd visited my class, she was dressed in a long skirt — this time a black-and-white print rather than solid black — and an oversized shirt. She even had on the same pendant she'd worn, a large gold four-leaf clover.

I must not have reacted quickly enough, because she repeated, "I'm here to see Mr. Cates. He called me and asked me to come over."

"I'll tell him," I said. Logan continued to straighten the plastic while Alex helped.

I knocked on the door to Mr. Cates's office. "Enter!" he called.

"There's a woman here — Professor Kingsolver — who says you called her," I said.

"She's here? Already?" Mr. Cates looked surprised. "That was quick."

"I told you she's always been interested in the connection between Poe and Gable," Mr. Gable said. "She can tell you a lot about what *she* thinks happened between them."

"Cillia will want to hear this too." Mr. Cates pushed his chair away from his desk and stood up. "Mary Anne, will you please tell Ms. Spark that the professor is here? By the way, this is Mr. Gable. His family owned this house for years, until we bought it for the store."

"Nice to meet you," I said. "Alex told us a little bit about Benson Dalton Gable already."

"He's very interested in the man," said Mr. Gable. "But then, it's an interesting story."

I wondered what he meant. I hoped they would stay in the main room to talk to Professor Kingsolver. I wanted to hear everything. I started to follow Mr. Cates and Mr. Gable, then remembered that I was supposed to find Ms. Spark and ask her to join them.

Mal and Kristy were absorbed in unpacking boxes and checking titles off a list. They looked up when I entered but didn't even stop when I told Ms. Spark that Mr. Cates wanted her to join him in the front of the store.

"Poe was approaching the end of his life and was despondent," Professor Kingsolver was saying as Ms. Spark and I joined the group. Logan was on a ladder painting away near the ceiling. "He'd failed at business after business. His writing never reached the levels of popularity he'd hoped for. His personal life was a mess. From some mentions in correspondence I've seen, I gather he and Gable began to exchange letters about writing. Gable also had aspirations of starting a magazine and Poe, I think, looked at this idea as another chance of reaching his dream. Evidently, Gable was one of the people who did have a healthy respect for Poe's work and Poe certainly basked in that, since it was rare enough." When Professor Kingsolver talked about Poe, she changed. She stood taller, her face lit up, and her voice sounded almost musical.

I picked up my paintbrush and worked on the lower part of the wall, leaving the high space to Logan.

"I'm not sure you're entirely right about that," said Alex.

Everyone turned to look at him. I couldn't imagine someone who was a student in high school challenging a college professor!

"Gable was a renowned mystery writer himself. Why do you assume that he started the relationship by worshipping Poe?" Alex asked.

"I don't think I said worship," Professor Kingsolver said. "I said respect."

"Perhaps Poe admired Gable," Alex said.

"He may have. In fact, I would say that their relationship probably was one of mutual respect."

Alex shook his head. "I think Poe knew that Gable was a far superior writer and was jealous of him. I think Poe started the correspondence, hoping to benefit from Gable's advice. And when Gable's work grew more popular than his, Poe began to resent him. Poe even stole ideas from Gable." Alex marched over to the fireplace, ducking under the ladder, and swept the plastic aside. I backed away. "Come here," he said.

Professor Kingsolver carefully skirted the ladder. She put one hand on her hip and shook her finger at Alex. "You should never walk under a ladder. Don't you know it's bad luck?" Then she laughed nervously as she patted the four-leaf clover pendant.

"Alex, I'm not sure Professor Kingsolver wants to listen to your theories about Poe and Gable," said his father.

"No, please. I'm interested in any insights as to the relationship between these two men," said the professor. "We don't have any substantive information about it, and I'm always looking for evidence of what it was. For example, I have often thought that Gable may have acted as an editor on some of Poe's manuscripts, but I can't find any solid evidence that they had this type of relationship."

Alex pointed at the carving on the fireplace. "Look here. Clearly, this is where Poe received his inspiration for 'The Raven.' "

We crowded around, trying to look at what Alex was indicating. I let Professor Kingsolver and Mr. Cates see first, then Ms. Spark and I took their places. A series of ravens was carved into the mantel. I wasn't quite sure that I followed Alex's argument. Even if Poe had been inspired by the carvings to write "The Raven," it wasn't the same thing as stealing ideas.

"The poem was published in 1845," said Professor Kingsolver. "Poe may have known Gable then. But I'm quite sure that the poem had its genesis in more than a carving on a fireplace mantel," she continued, echoing my thoughts.

"Benson Dalton Gable mentions ravens in his work often," said Alex. "I've read every word he's ever written — every word we've been able to find. Poe was an idea thief. And what if Gable threatened to expose him? Poe had a penchant for writing about revenge and murder. Maybe it grew out of his own feelings."

"Alex, that's enough. I think you're going a little too far with that," said Mr. Gable.

What exactly did Alex mean about revenge and murder and Benson Dalton Gable? Did Poe take some sort of revenge on Gable? Or Gable on Poe? I didn't remember reading or hearing anything like that.

"That *does* go a little far," Professor Kingsolver put in. "Poe was quite capable of coming up with such ideas from the depths of his tortured psyche. He was a very unhappy creature, as is evident in his work."

I felt a tickle around my ankles and looked down. Pluto was circling my legs, rubbing against my ankles. I reached down and gave him a pat on his head, and he moved on to Professor Kingsolver. As soon as he touched her ankle, she jumped back. Pluto darted between her feet and into the hallway.

"A black cat! Mr. Cates, you must intend to make a success of this store, yet you're asking for bad luck with that cat on the premises," Professor Kingsolver said, once she'd regained her composure. Now she was grasping her pendant tightly, holding on as if for dear life.

"That's Pluto," said Mr. Cates, a smile playing about his lips. "And he's a part of the family — not always a willing part of the family, but loved anyway."

"I would never deliberately welcome a black cat into my home," said Professor Kingsolver. "And as for your theory, young man," she said, turning to Alex, "you have a good mind, but you seem to be fixated on the relative merits of the writing of Gable and Poe. It's obvious that Poe is the superior talent. His work is revered still."

The voice Professor Kingsolver used here must have been the one she used with students in her classroom. I found myself doing a lot more than painting.

"But do we know the extent of Gable's work?" Alex challenged. "We know only what we've found. Perhaps someone destroyed the better part of it."

Professor Kingsolver shook her head.

"This is quite interesting," said Mr. Cates. "I had no idea there was any indication that Gable and Poe feuded."

"There isn't," Professor Kingsolver said quickly.

"Only what we can suppose," said Alex.

"I think everyone has had enough of your theories for today," Mr. Gable said to Alex. "I'm sure Mr. Cates and his crew need to get back to work."

I noticed that one of the workmen had come in while Professor Kingsolver and Alex were talking. He'd only installed one switch plate from an entire stack since he'd arrived. His ear was turned to the speakers and seemed to be listening to the conversation. In other words, he'd done as much work as I had.

"Check our umbrellas and see if they're dry yet," Mr. Gable said to Alex.

Alex opened the door and pulled in two of the umbrellas I'd seen resting on the porch. He dropped one on the floor and held the other in front of him, preparing to open it.

"NO! Stop!" Professor Kingsolver grabbed the umbrella. "It's bad luck to open an umbrella inside the house. You people are asking for it."

Professor Kingsolver was the most superstitious adult I'd ever met. The ladder, the black cat, the four-leaf clover, and now the umbrella. Where was the rabbit's foot? I glanced at her purse. Her keys hung off a rabbit's foot keychain hooked on the strap of her bag.

I could tell that Logan wanted to laugh. His eyes were sparkling as he leaned over the can of primer, stirring again. Ms. Spark and Mr. Cates both looked as if they might burst out laughing any minute too.

"I must go as well," said Professor Kingsolver, "but be assured that I'd be glad to consult with you at any time about Poe. I'm delighted you've decided to locate your establishment in our town. If you ever need any advice about anything you might find, please call me."

"Thank you for coming by," said Mr. Cates.

"A pleasure to meet you," said Ms. Spark.

"I'll call you when I have the rest of the papers," Mr. Gable said to Mr. Cates. He held the door for Professor Kingsolver.

"Work hard," Alex said as he dashed into the rain.

As soon as the door shut, Mr. Cates and Ms. Spark started laughing. Even the workman wore a grin.

"She's something else," said Mr. Cates.

"Poor Pluto! He's in trouble whether he's crabby or simply trying to be friendly," said Ms. Spark.

"But what they had to say about Poe and Gable was very interesting, don't you think?" said Mr. Cates.

"I don't understand why Alex is so sure that Poe was jealous of Gable," I said, my curiosity piqued.

"I don't quite either," said Mr. Cates. "Perhaps he's simply defending his ancestor. He's certainly interested in the history surrounding him and Poe."

I could see why. I was interested too, and I wasn't related to either one.

"I'm going to help the girls with the books," said Ms. Spark.

"And I'll grab a paintbrush," said Mr. Cates.

We worked through the afternoon. Kristy and Mal, with Ms. Spark's help, checked in boxes of books. Mal and I were glad that there was going to be a children's section, including Nancy Drews for Claudia. There were also copies of one of my favorites, *The Westing Game*, and one of Mal's favorites, *From the*

Mixed-Up Files of Mrs. Basil E. Frankweiler. Of course, there were lots of others we hadn't read yet and were itching to dig into.

"You girls sound as if you know what you're talking about," Ms. Spark said, listening in as Mal and I discussed some of the titles while we waited for Logan and Mr. Cates to finish cleaning the paintbrushes.

"I like to read," said Mal.

"Me too."

"You know, Mal and Mary Anne and the rest of us could write little descriptions of some of the books we like a lot and you could post them. It would be a way to give customers a recommendation," said Kristy.

"What a great idea!" said Ms. Spark. "I'll tell Larry about it. Would you really want to do this?"

"I'd love to," said Mal. I nodded in agreement.

"Sure," said Kristy.

"I need to pick up the kids at the pizza parlor. They're going to think I forgot them," said Mr. Cates, rushing into the main room. "I'd be glad to give you girls a ride home."

"I need to pick up a prescription I called in to the pharmacy before it closes," said Ms. Spark, "so I need to leave too. Who wants to ride with me?"

Logan had followed Mr. Cates and joined us

by the front door. Kristy and Mal decided to go with Mr. Cates, leaving Logan and me to ride with Ms. Spark.

"Wait a minute," said Ms. Spark. "We can't all go. There's one more delivery to come today. The computer monitor, to replace the one that wouldn't turn on. It's coming express. It's supposed to be here by five." She looked at her watch.

"I'll stay until you come back," I offered.

"You will?" asked Mr. Cates. "Cillia and I haven't been out of here for more than five minutes all day. It would be a nice break for us. If the workmen hadn't already left, I'm sure one of them would let the deliveryman in, but they seemed pretty anxious to be gone for some reason. I'll drive you home as soon as we get back."

"I'll stay with Mary Anne," said Logan.

I turned and smiled at him.

"Wait just a minute," said Mr. Cates, feeling around in his pockets. "I need to check something." He disappeared down the hallway.

"You'll ride in the van, the white one with the raven on the door," Ms. Spark said to Kristy and Mal. "Let's go on out."

"See you Monday," I said.

"See you," said Logan.

Mal and Kristy pulled their hoods over their heads and dashed to the van. Ms. Spark grabbed her purse and followed, opening her umbrella as soon as she was outside the door. She climbed into the black Toyota parked near the van.

"Be back soon," called Mr. Cates, following them through the rain.

Logan started folding up the plastic sheets. I decided to go back to the receiving room, but before I even reached the hall there was a knock on the door.

"Delivery!" a voice called.

Logan unlocked the door and opened it. A man staggered inside carrying a bulky box.

"Back here," I said, showing him the way to Mr. Cates's office, where he'd told us to have the monitor left.

"Last delivery," the man said. "I can go home and dry out a little now."

"Good night," I said, closing and locking the door behind him.

"That was quick," I said to Logan. "They must have passed the delivery truck on their way down the street."

"Well, I guess we'll just wait for Mr. Cates to come back," said Logan. He followed me into the receiving room.

"Look at this leather-bound edition of Edgar Allan Poe stories." I handed the book to Logan. It was black with gold letters on the front cover and spine.

"It smells good," Logan said, handing it back. "And it's beautiful. It looks like a book people put on a shelf, but never read."

He was probably right.

The rain sounded a little louder in this room, I thought as I picked up another Poe book, a volume of poetry. "Logan, do you hear anything?" I asked, the hairs on the back of my neck feeling prickly.

"Rain," he said.

"No, not rain." Fluh-dub, fluh-dub, fluh-dub. It wasn't the drip, drip, drip of water. My mouth suddenly felt dry as I looked over my shoulder into the dark hallway. I squinted, but still saw nothing. The sound seemed to grow louder until I could feel as well as hear it.

"It's a heart — the tell-tale heart," I whispered, moving close to Logan. He put his arm around me. My own heart was pounding as if in echo.

"I hear it," he said, "but it can't be a heart, Mary Anne. It must be water from someplace."

"Listen." I put my finger over my lips. Gradually the beating sound grew softer and softer, then disappeared. It was replaced by the sound of dripping water.

"See, it's gone now," said Logan, squeezing my shoulders.

"But drips don't suddenly stop," I said. "Where do you think it was coming from?" I didn't really want to leave the room we were in.

"The roof," said Logan, "or maybe the basement."

Basements were so dark and scary. What if —

"We're back!" The front door opened and the Cateses entered. Ms. Spark followed. I was surprised to see her. I hadn't expected her to come back that night. She certainly worked hard.

Logan and I joined them. "How was the movie?" I asked Tom and Gillian.

"Fine," said Gillian. "Claudia's nice."

"Can I go to my room now?" Tom asked.

"Yes, and don't come out until I say you can," said Mr. Cates.

Ms. Spark stayed by the door. "I'll stop by tomorrow," she said.

"You don't have to go yet," said Mr. Cates. "I'm so sorry Tom was rude to you."

"I think I should leave. Tom seems upset. Maybe you need some family time together."

For a moment I thought Mr. Cates was going to kiss Ms. Spark, but he didn't. Maybe she hadn't come back to work after all.

"I'll drive Mary Anne and Logan home," she offered.

"Thanks," Mr. Cates said. "Is that okay with you two?"

I wondered if I should mention the heartbeat. Now that we were in the brightly lit main room with people all around, I wasn't sure I'd heard anything unusual. Still, if there was a drip, Mr. Cates should know.

"We heard something strange while you were gone," I said.

"Old houses have lots of strange noises, don't they, Gillian?" Mr. Cates said. He kept looking toward the stairs. "You go on up and pick out a game we can play together."

" 'Bye, Mary Anne. 'Bye, Mary Anne's boyfriend," Gillian said, running from the room, giggling.

"Claudia told her that's who Logan is," said Mr. Cates, also grinning.

"The noise," I said. "It sounded like . . . you're going to think I'm crazy, but it sounded like a beating heart." I rushed the last part, then looked to Logan for support.

"It did sort of sound like that," he said.

"It must have been water dripping. There's a place in the basement where water keeps coming in. I'll have some of the guys check it out on Monday," Mr. Cates said. "But Mary Anne, I think a little of our obsession with Poe is starting to rub off on you. Did you know that he wrote a story —"

" — 'The Tell-Tale Heart,' " I said, finishing his sentence.

"Exactly," said Mr. Cates. "So you *are* a fan."

"We're studying mysteries in English and I'm doing a project on Poe."

"Good choice!"

As we drove away from Poe and Co., I looked back at the house. Dark clouds swirled around it and a flash of lightning split the sky directly above it, lighting the darkened windows for a second. The house seemed almost to throb when the thunder cracked, like a beating heart. I shivered, and not from the chill of the rain.

CHAPTER 5

Rain, rain, go away — and do'nt bother to come back annother day. Saterday I baby-sat for Tom and Jilian Kates. Tom did'nt want to be baby-sat and he was'nt shy about teling me. But, that was'nt the wurst thing. The wurest thing is that everybudy in the hole werld is tired of rain. And there geting testy.

I mentioned to the rest of the BSC members (I wrote it in the notebook too) that I thought Tom and Gillian Cates might be playing tricks on Ms. Spark (although I had no proof), that the kids definitely didn't want to live in Stoneybrook, and that they weren't over the fact that their mother had left. Tom in particular seemed to want to keep people at a distance, and this rubbed off on Gillian. Claudia said she thought the rain was responsible for the terrible afternoon they'd had at the movies and later at Pizza Express. It was probably a combination of everything.

Stacey was sitting for Charlotte Johanssen that day. They joined Claudia and the Cates kids at the movie. Claud and Stacey thought Gillian and Charlotte might enjoy each other's company.

Stacey and Charlotte were waiting in the lobby of the theater when Claudia, Tom, and Gillian arrived. Claudia hadn't been able to talk much with Tom and Gillian on the way to the movie. Mr. Cates drove them, and anytime the kids didn't answer Claud's questions right away, he answered for them, just the way he had when I sat on Thursday. But Claudia knew they'd be on their own after he dropped them off, and they'd have to talk eventually.

"Claudia! Over here!" Stacey and Charlotte

were standing at the entrance to the theater showing *Star Wars*, the movie they'd agreed to see.

"Stacey, Charlotte, meet Tom and Gillian Cates. Tom and Gillian's dad is opening a mystery bookstore," Claudia said.

"Hi," Charlotte said, smiling and showing her dimples.

"Hi," said Stacey.

Tom looked all around and didn't respond.

"It's nice to meet you," Gillian said shyly.

"This is one of my favorite movies," said Stacey. "Have either of you seen it? Charlotte and I watched it on her VCR once, but we've never seen it on the big screen together."

"Of course we've seen it," said Tom. "Who hasn't seen *Star Wars*?"

"Snacks anybody?" Claudia asked.

"I think I'll have a diet soda," said Stacey. "You want anything, Charlotte?"

"Can I get popcorn?" Charlotte asked.

The group moved over to the line at the candy counter.

"I think I'll have M&Ms," said Claudia. "No, maybe I'll have Sno-caps. That big Crunch bar looks good too."

"Go ahead — buy them all!" Stacey teased.

"What would you like?" Claudia asked Tom and Gillian.

"Nothing," said Tom.

Gillian looked at her brother, then at the candy in the display case. "Nothing, I guess," she said softly.

"I'll buy a big box of M&Ms, and if you decide you want some later, I'll share," said Claudia.

Gillian nodded.

"Let's play video games before we go in and sit down," said Tom.

"We don't have time. Later, when we go for pizza, you can play there."

Tom scowled and crossed his arms.

Claudia and Stacey paid for the snacks. Then Claudia pushed the door of the theater open and held it while everyone passed in front of her. She smiled down at Tom and Gillian as they walked by. As soon as she stepped inside the theater, Claudia was bombarded with kernels of popcorn.

"Stop it!" Claudia heard a loud whisper as she looked around to see where the little missiles had come from. Mrs. Pike was taking buckets of popcorn away from Jordan, Byron, and Adam. Vanessa and Margo were waving at Stacey and Claudia.

"Let's sit behind the Pikes," Claudia said to Stacey, thinking that the triplets might be good company for Tom. She didn't want to sit in front of them and serve as a target for secret popcorn practice. (Mrs. Pike was bound to return their popcorn at some point.)

"Hi, girls," Mallory's mother greeted them. "I left the kids for one second to go to the bathroom and they decided to stage a guerrilla popcorn attack. And," she turned to the triplets, "if it happens again, the popcorn is history permanently."

"Sorry, Claudia," Jordan said.

"You didn't hit me that many times," said Claudia. "Do you guys know Tom Cates?"

"Hi, Tom," said Byron. "He's in my class," he added to Claudia.

"You all look alike," said Gillian.

"We're identical triplets," said Adam.

"Does your mom know which one is which?" she asked.

"Usually," said Mrs. Pike with a smile.

"This is Gillian Cates," said Claudia.

"She's in my class at school," said Margo. "Hi, Gill."

"It's Gillian," said Tom.

"This is Mrs. Pike, Vanessa, and Margo." Claudia finished the introductions. "Where are Nicky and Claire?"

"At home with their dad," said Mrs. Pike.

Jordan punched Adam, and Mrs. Pike made him change seats with her.

"I need to go to the bathroom," said Tom.

"Gillian, please stay here with Stacey. Come on, Tom." Claudia stood up.

"I'm not a baby. You don't have to go with me," he said.

"I'm not going *into* the bathroom with you. I'll wait outside. I need a drink of water to wash the M&Ms down anyway."

Tom sighed, then stood up and walked quickly down the aisle. The door to the men's room was swinging shut before Claudia stepped into the lobby. She took a long drink of water, then leaned against the wall across from the bathroom.

The music signaling the coming attractions started. Claudia paced a few steps in one direction, then turned and retraced her path. She stared at the men's room door. She opened the door to the theater and saw that the lights had gone down and the preview was starting.

A man walked out of the bathroom. Claudia thought maybe Tom had had to wait.

She stood there a little longer, until she heard the music for the main feature. Tom was taking a long time. Maybe he was sick. How could she check? No one with a theater uniform was in sight. Claudia braced herself and approached the door to the men's room. She knocked. "Tom?" she called softly.

The door opened. "You looking for someone?"

Claudia felt her face grow hot. It was Alan Gray! Why couldn't it have been anyone but him? Alan was also in the eighth grade at SMS and when he wasn't playing jokes on people, he was planning tricks or talking about things that were embarrassing to others. By Monday afternoon everybody at SMS would know that she had knocked on the door of the men's bathroom. "Would you check to see if there's a boy in there? His name is Tom," said Claudia, trying to stay calm.

"I was the only one in there," said Alan.

"I know he's in there. Please go check. It's been so long I'm worried he might be sick."

Alan went back inside, then yelled loudly enough for Claudia to hear, "Tom! There's a Claudia Kishi waiting outside the door for you! She really likes you!"

There was no answer. Alan returned alone.

"Tom is someone I'm baby-sitting for," Claudia said. "He's not a boyfriend."

"That's okay, Claud. This will be between you and me." Alan laughed as he walked away.

"Thanks," Claudia called after him. Suddenly she had an inspiration. She ran to the lobby and there was Tom, playing video games.

Claudia took him by the arm. "I said we'd play later. The movie's started." She steered him toward the theater.

"I'm not finished," Tom said. "Besides, I've already seen the movie a million times."

"Tom, we're going into the movie now," Claudia said firmly.

Again he sighed. Instead of going to the theater, Tom opened the door to the bathroom. "I didn't use the bathroom yet," he whined.

Claudia waited, her arms crossed, until he came out. She followed him back into the auditorium and to his seat.

"What took you so long?" Stacey whispered.

"Tell you later," said Claudia.

"Might as well tell me now. There's so much talking, you can't hear anyway," said Stacey.

All around them, kids talked and laughed. Popcorn, ice, cups, and candy wrappers flew through the air. Tom leaned back in his seat, closed his eyes, and snored. Claudia knew he couldn't have fallen asleep that fast. Gillian scooted a little closer to her and gave her a shy smile. Claudia smiled back.

By the end of the movie, Claudia had a headache from all the noise. She'd had to duck several times to avoid being hit with flying objects. The M&Ms hadn't lasted nearly long enough, and she was ready for pizza.

As they were walking out of the theater, the Pikes close behind them, Tom said, loudly enough for everyone to hear, "It is so juvenile to come to the movies with your *mom*."

Claudia placed a hand on Tom's shoulder and speeded up the pace.

They walked around the corner and through the drizzle to Pizza Express. Tom led the way (with Claudia giving him directions), Gillian and Charlotte walked together, not saying much, and Claudia and Stacey brought up the rear. Lots of people had had the same idea. Claudia told me later that she felt as if she were part of a herd. People were in front of them, behind them, and even crowding past them.

Claudia paused inside the entrance, searching for a place to sit. Somehow the Pikes had reached Pizza Express first and commandeered a large table.

"Come on over here," Margo shouted. "We have plenty of room."

"Do we have to?" Tom asked.

"If we don't, we'll have to wait," said Claudia, "and I don't know about you, but I'm hungry." They worked their way through the tables, followed by Stacey and Charlotte. Tom stood in the entryway for a moment, then followed too, his head down.

Mrs. Pike sat at one end of the table, with Byron and Jordan on either side of her. Vanessa sat next to Byron, Margo between Jordan and Adam. The boys were arguing about what kind of pizza to order. Mrs. Pike was massaging her temples.

"Hi, Claudia! Hi, Stacey!" Karen Brewer, Kristy's seven-year-old stepsister, patted each girl on the head as she passed by.

"Hi, Karen, Andrew, Mrs. Engle," Claudia said as they squeezed through, heading for a small table in the corner at the rear of the restaurant. Andrew is Karen's younger brother; Mrs. Engle is their mother.

Byron folded his napkin into a paper airplane and sailed it toward the far end of the table where Tom sat. The napkin only made it as far as Adam, who picked it up and threw it a little farther. Claudia picked it up and returned it. They passed the airplane back and forth, until Tom grabbed it and wadded the napkin into a ball. He threw the ball at Byron and it hit Mrs. Pike.

"Tom, please apologize to Mrs. Pike," Claudia said.

"Sorry," Tom mumbled, folding his arms and looking down.

"I think you all need to stand up awhile," said Mrs. Pike. She grabbed her purse and pulled out her billfold. "Here, go play video games while we're waiting for the pizza."

Tom stayed in his seat.

"You want to go too?" Claudia asked him.

Tom shook his head.

"At the theater you wanted to play video

games more than you wanted to see the movie."

"There aren't any good ones here," said Tom. "We had really good games at the arcade I used to go to. My mom used to let me play for hours. She would bring rolls of quarters when we went there."

"That must have been fun," said Claudia. "Which game is your favorite?"

"I like all of them. Except the ones they have here," he added quickly.

"That's too bad. Your dad gave me quarters in case you wanted to play."

"Maybe later," said Tom.

"Am I getting old or is it very noisy in here?" Mrs. Pike asked.

"It's pretty noisy," Stacey said. She'd given the girls a pencil and they were passing it around as they played ticktacktoe on napkins.

"Two in a row, one more to go," Vanessa said.

"Claudia, did your new boyfriend ever come out of the bathroom?" Alan Gray asked, stopping at their table.

Claudia scowled. "This is Tom Cates. His dad is opening a bookstore in the old Gable house. I'm baby-sitting for him and his sister, Gillian."

"Whatever you say." Alan joined a table of eighth-grade boys.

"What boyfriend? Who is he talking about?" Stacey asked.

"It's a long story."

"Alan Gray's so irritating," said Stacey.

"Tell me about it."

A small roar came from the video arcade. Mrs. Pike rushed to see what was going on. An older kid had cut in line in front of Adam. Adam tried to explain that he'd been waiting, but the boy had pushed him. Adam's brothers protested and some friends of the older boy joined him. Soon everyone was shouting and pushing.

After Mrs. Pike and some other mothers separated the boys, they returned to the table. The pizzas arrived at the same time.

"No wonder they have to stay with their mom," said Tom.

Tom and Gillian ate their pizza without even a pause. Claudia had hoped they'd make it last until Mr. Cates arrived, but they didn't.

"My cheese is in bed, a bed of red, it's soft and chewy, stretchy and gooey," Vanessa rhymed.

"Does she always talk like that?" Gillian whispered to Claudia.

"Only some of the time," said Claudia. "She wants to be a poet."

As soon as they were finished eating, Mrs. Pike rounded up her family and left.

As more people left, a few at a time, the noise level gradually decreased. After Stacey and Charlotte left, Tom decided he would play video games. Gillian stood close by him, watching.

Claudia breathed a sigh of relief when the restaurant quieted down. She couldn't wait to get home.

CHAPTER 6

I'd agreed to return to Poe and Co. on Monday to help.

"More of the BSC to meet?" Ms. Spark asked when I entered with Abby, Stacey, and Claudia. "I do know Claudia, from Saturday."

I introduced the rest of my friends to her.

"Uh-oh," said Abby. "I feel by dose stoppig up already."

"I don't think we can open the windows with the rain and everything," I said. "Abby's allergic to paint," I explained to Ms. Spark.

"Maybe you should go upstairs and supervise Tom and Gillian," she suggested. "Larry hasn't even thought about painting anything up there yet."

"That's great," said Abby.

"And Claudia, Mary Anne mentioned that you're the artist in the group. Is there any chance you could paint some trim on this wall?" Ms. Spark pointed at the white wall Logan and I had primed on Saturday.

"I guess it depends on what you want me to paint," said Claudia.

"Let me take care of some other jobs and then we'll talk about some ideas I have," Ms. Spark said. "Mary Anne, would you take Abby upstairs and introduce her to Tom and Gillian? Let's see, what else do we need? Stacey, would you like to check in more books? I'll show you what to do."

"Abby, let's go upstairs and meet Tom and Gillian," I said. "Then I'll come back and help Stacey."

"Good, by dose is really stuffy," said Abby, sniffing.

At the top of the stairs I called Tom and Gillian.

"We're in the living room," Gillian answered.

I followed the sound of her voice.

"It used to be a bedroom," Tom said when we entered the room.

"Nice," said Abby.

"This is Abby Stevenson. She's going to stay up here with you guys this afternoon," I explained.

"Another baby-sitter?" said Tom. He turned and stared at the television.

Gillian smiled at Abby. "Do you know how

to play Hi, Ho Cherry-O?" she asked. "We have that game."

"Where's my dad?" asked Tom. "I don't want to stay up here with girls all afternoon."

"He's busy," Abby said.

Ouch, I thought. That's probably the last thing he wants to hear.

"Pretty soon the store will open and things will settle down a little," I added.

"Right," said Tom, looking at me as if I had three eyes.

"I'll be downstairs if you need anything," I said to Abby.

As I came down the steps, I heard a familiar but unexpected voice.

"Those boxes must be heavy." What was Alex Gable doing back here? I wondered.

He was in the receiving room, lifting boxes onto the table beside Stacey.

"Hi, Alex," I greeted him.

"Hi. You were here on Saturday. Mary Anne, right?"

"Right. I see you've met Stacey. She's in the BSC too," I told him.

Alex had hoisted a box halfway to the table when it slipped out of his hands and books tumbled across the floor. "You are?" His eyes grew large as he stared at Stacey. "I thought I'd seen you at Stoneybrook High."

"I'm thirteen, just like Mary Anne," said Stacey, smiling.

"You're sure?" Alex asked, glancing at me.

Did he think we were kidding him?

Stacey assured him she was thirteen as we gathered the loose books and stacked them on one end of the table.

"Is Mr. Cates here? Or are you in charge?" Again, Alex turned to Stacey. He leaned forward, resting his arm on the table and smiled broadly.

Alex Gable was flirting with Stacey! It somehow made him seem a lot more like other high school boys.

"Mr. Cates is here," Stacey answered.

"And Ms. Spark," I added. "They're in the office."

"I'm picking up some papers for my dad. There wasn't anyone in the front room, only workmen in Benson Dalton Gable's office, and then I found Stacey." Again, Alex smiled at her. "Have you seen the entire house yet?" he asked.

"Today's my first day on the job. But Mary Anne's been here a couple of times," said Stacey.

"You haven't seen anything . . . odd, have you?" Alex asked me.

"Odd? What do you mean?"

"Just how much do you know about Benson Dalton Gable?" Alex asked.

"Just that he used to live here," said Stacey.

Not as much as I want to, I thought. "Only what you talked about last Saturday," I answered.

"Did you know that there's a mystery surrounding his death?" Alex said in a low voice.

Stacey and I shook our heads. I moved a little closer to Stacey.

"For one thing, no one knows for sure when he died because we've never been able to find his grave. And Poe was one of his last-known visitors." Alex grinned, watching us closely.

"Have you ever read any of Poe's stories? 'The Cask of Amontillado?' 'The Tell-Tale Heart'?" he asked.

I felt cold and rubbed my arms. "I have," I answered. Stacey shook her head again.

"Then you know what they're about. In both stories, one man kills another and hides the body. Behind a wall, under the floor. Actually, in 'The Cask of Amontillado,' he doesn't even bother to kill the man first. He walls him up alive."

I wouldn't want to be around a campfire with Alex Gable telling ghost stories. What he said and the way he said it gave me goosebumps.

Stacey moved a little closer to me. "Do you

think the house is haunted?" she asked. It was just what I was thinking. "Could his body still be," Stacey looked around, "here?"

Alex shrugged. "Who knows? Many of his papers vanished too. And that happened around the time of his death. The two could be connected. Dad and I would like to publish a collection of his work, but there are too many gaps. I've looked everywhere in the house, but I keep thinking that with all the construction, maybe something will turn up. You haven't seen anything, have you?"

"Nope," I said.

"Keep your eyes open and give me a call if you do," said Alex — to Stacey, not to me.

"Mr. Cates is in his office," I said. "Knock if you need to see him."

"Thanks." Alex smiled at Stacey one last time, then left.

"He's a cheery person to have around," said Stacey. "Now I feel like I may be walking on top of Benson Dalton Gable every time I take a step."

"That's an interesting notion," I said. "I wonder if there's anything to back up Alex's theory, or if his imagination is working overtime."

"I don't have a clue."

"Well, let's get to work," I said.

We'd checked in two boxes of books when I heard a commotion in the hall.

"Tom, you said you were going to the kitchen for a snack," I heard Abby say.

"Be back in a minute," I said to Stacey.

"I did. Look." When I joined them, Tom was holding out a handful of cookies.

"You know you aren't supposed to bother your dad," Abby continued. "Please go back upstairs."

"What happened?" I asked as Tom disappeared at the top of the stairway.

"Tom came downstairs to eat a snack, which I thought was okay, but he was gone so long, I came down to check. I found him in the office with his dad and Ms. Spark."

"Go back upstairs before you're all stuffed up again," I said. "Is everything else all right?"

"Tom and Gillian spend more time whispering to each other than they do talking to me, but it's okay," said Abby, heading for the stairs.

As I passed Benson Dalton Gable's old office, I saw someone leaning over the desk. "Professor Kingsolver?" I asked.

"Hello," she said quickly, straightening up. "I couldn't seem to find anyone but workmen around."

"Mr. Cates is in his office," I said. I looked around the room. It had undergone a slight change since the last time I'd been in there. The old wall had been ripped away, and new drywall installed. It hadn't been primed yet — a job for Logan.

"I've often imagined Poe and Gable sitting across from one another at this desk. See, it has places for two people to sit." Professor Kingsolver showed me the kneeholes on each side. "They would be discussing writing, maybe even exchanging manuscripts." She looked around the room as she ran her hand over the desk slowly.

Meow. Meeeeooooow.

Professor Kingsolver jumped and moved a few steps backward, toward the door. I knelt down to search for Pluto. He sounded scared. I couldn't see him, though.

I heard a scratching sound across the room.

"Where is he?" Professor Kingsolver said in a shaky voice.

"It sounds as if he's over there," I said, pointing. The cat meowed again as I stared at the new drywall. He sounded nearby, yet muffled. Then I remembered the story, "The Black Cat," and how the cat had ended up trapped behind the wall. It crawled in while the husband was hiding his murdered wife's body. A chill settled over me. Did I want to find the cat?

The meows became more frantic. I *had* to find him. As soon as I pressed my ear against the raw wallboard, the meows stopped. Could

Pluto really have gotten *behind* the wall? Maybe he was trapped in a neighboring room.

"Maybe he's closed up in the room next door," I said to Professor Kingsolver. "I'll check."

Professor Kingsolver followed me into the hallway.

I paused and looked up and down what now seemed a dim, dark tunnel instead of the formerly inviting hall. No cat. No meows.

There was only one door near Benson Dalton Gable's office. I opened it and the meows resumed. It was a small closet, and remembering what had happened to Ms. Spark my first day on the job, I stepped back quickly expecting the cat to jump out. He didn't.

The kitchen was on the other side of the office, but after a quick check, I realized that the meowing couldn't have come from there. Appliances lined the wall between the kitchen and Gable's office.

"Did you find the cat?" Professor Kingsolver asked as I returned to the hall.

"Not yet." I tried to smile.

I stood at the door to the office and examined each wall carefully. The meows resumed, again seeming to come from behind the new drywall. "Pluto. Here, kitty," I called softly. I tapped on the wall.

A scratch and a meow answered my call. I

decided it was time to tell Mr. Cates what might have happened.

I ran the short distance down the hall to his office and knocked on the door.

"Enter!" he called.

"I'm sorry to bother you, but I think Pluto is trapped behind the wall in Benson Dalton Gable's office," I said breathlessly.

Mr. Cates and Ms. Spark stood up quickly and followed me to the small room.

The cat was howling now. The noise had drawn Stacey into the hallway and she stood beside Professor Kingsolver.

"What is that?" asked Stacey.

"I think the cat's behind the wall," I explained.

Ms. Spark summoned one of the workmen, and he and Mr. Cates used a small axe to knock a hole in the fresh wallboard well above Pluto. The workman reached inside the hole and ripped the new drywall away from the studs.

As soon as the opening was big enough, Pluto jumped out and ran away.

Pluto must have crawled inside after the old wall was torn away and was still there when the new wall was nailed into place. No wonder he was upset!

"I'll fix this right away," the workman said to Mr. Cates. "I never would have thought to see if a cat was in there, before I finished up."

"Thanks, Andy," Mr. Cates answered.

"This is the oddest place," said Professor Kingsolver. "There are some very strange things going on here. That black cat . . . walled up, just like in the Poe story."

Professor Kingsolver was saying out loud what I was thinking. And she didn't even know about the sound of the beating heart.

"I think this house is haunted," Professor Kingsolver burst out.

"I hope not," Mr. Cates said, laughing nervously. "I've sunk my life savings into this place, and if a ghost scares away my customers, I'm in big trouble."

"That won't happen. It's all coincidence," said Ms. Spark, patting Mr. Cates's arm as she glared at the professor.

"Did you — did you find that drip I heard Saturday?" I asked.

"Drip?"

"The sound Logan and I heard, while you were gone," I said. "Like a —"

"Oh, yeah!" he said before I could go any further. "No, we looked, but we didn't find a thing."

The first thing I did at the BSC meeting that afternoon was pull out the mystery notebook. We use it to keep track of clues when we're involved in a mystery. (We've solved quite a few.) I thought that there were definitely mysterious things happening at Poe and Co.

I listed everyone we'd met at the store so far: Ms. Spark, Professor Kingsolver, Alex Gable, and his father. I added Mr. Cates, Tom, and Gillian. Who in this group might be behind the strange happenings and why?

Kristy didn't give me a chance to finish what I intended to write down. "What are you doing?" she asked as I stared at the list of names, thinking.

"So many weird things have happened at Poe and Co. I thought it was time to start keeping a record," I said.

"A mystery!" said Abby. "I have a question. Where is Mrs. Cates?"

"I don't know," I answered. "All Mr. Cates said was that she left. And Tom and Gillian seem to be having trouble with it."

"They don't like Ms. Spark much, that's for sure," Abby said. "I think Tom wanted to see what they were doing in his dad's office and that's why he went in. Also, he made me a little nervous every time he and Gillian whispered together. I hope they weren't planning something else for Ms. Spark. She seems pretty nice to me."

"They could be trying to scare her away," Kristy said. "Remember the first day you sat for them? Tom shut the cat in the closet, and then told her to open the door."

"But how would they make the sound of that heartbeat?" I asked. "And would they know about the Poe stories?"

"Alex Gable seems to think there may be a dead body someplace in the Gable house. Benson Dalton Gable's body," said Stacey.

"No!" said Claudia. She'd spent the afternoon painting black ravens on the white walls in the front room. In the children's corner, she'd painted a silhouette of Nancy Drew with her magnifying glass, just like the picture on the covers of the old books.

"He said that no one knew where the body was buried," Stacey continued.

"Right. And he thinks there are still papers that belong to Gable hidden someplace in the house," I said.

"Maybe they're buried with him," said Mal.

Everyone shuddered. I felt as if a cold wind had blown through the room.

"I have a list of all the people who've been at the store when we've been there — and when strange things have happened or near the time they've happened," I said, holding it up.

"What kind of strange things?" asked Jessi.

I'd forgotten that Jessi hadn't had a chance to work at Poe and Co. yet.

"Like the cat jumping on Ms. Spark when she opened the closet door," said Stacey. "Probably Tom and Gillian were responsible for that."

"And the heartbeat I heard when Logan and I were there alone," I said.

"And finding a black cat trapped behind a wall," Mal added.

"Do you think the store might be," Stacey paused and lowered her voice, "haunted?"

"Or is all the talk about Edgar Allan Poe and his stories making us think it's haunted?" Kristy asked.

We were quiet for awhile. Jessi finally broke the silence. "I can't wait to go to the store now. I didn't know there was a mystery. I thought you were working."

"We are working, but there are lots of interruptions," said Mal.

"Like Professor Kingsolver, and Alex, and keeping the kids from running Ms. Spark out," said Stacey.

"Remember how superstitious Professor Kingsolver acted on Saturday?" said Mal.

I nodded.

"And how she and Alex argued over what kind of relationship Poe and Gable had?" Mal continued. "If Alex thinks there are papers hidden someplace in the house, maybe he doesn't want anybody else to find them — especially Professor Kingsolver. He could be trying to scare her away."

"I saw him coming up from the basement and looking around on Saturday. And today he was there before we found the cat," I said.

"I'd like to know how he rigged up something to sound like a beating heart," said Abby. "That seems like a lot of work."

Kristy looked over my shoulder at the list of suspects. "So why would Professor Kingsolver want to scare anyone away?" she asked.

"She's obsessed with Edgar Allan Poe," said Stacey. "But I can't think of any reason she would want to scare us, or anyone else, away from Poe and Co."

"Maybe we need to find out a little more about Alex and Professor Kingsolver," said Kristy. "He goes to Stoneybrook High, right?"

"I guess so," I answered.

"I'll ask my brothers if they know him."

"And I could ask Janine," said Claudia.

"Ask Janine about Professor Kingsolver, too," I said. "She teaches at Stoneybrook University."

"We need to keep an open mind about other suspects," Claudia said.

"You know," said Abby, "I've heard my mom talk about how competitive the bookstore business is now. Maybe someone doesn't want the store to open at all."

"Or maybe Alex doesn't want it to open in the Gable house," said Stacey.

"Maybe he's hoping Mr. Cates will be so spooked, he'll want to sell it back to the family," said Jessi.

"We need to pay close attention to all our suspects when we're at Poe and Co.," I said. "If we stay alert, we can figure this out."

"And stay clear of ghosts," said Abby, grinning.

"My turn to go tomorrow," said Jessi.

CHAPTER 7

"What's going on in there now?" Mal asked as she, Jessi, and I slogged through the mud to reach the front door of Poe and Co. The boards and brick had sunk, and mud was oozing over them, since it was still raining.

The sound of shouting had reached us before we started up the steps to the porch. I recognized Ms. Spark's voice.

"Should we go in?" Jessi asked.

"I guess so," I replied. I opened the door. Ms. Spark was standing in front of a group of workmen, telling them in a very loud voice (okay, she was yelling) that they weren't working fast enough. The opening was behind schedule and they were losing money every day.

"We can't control the weather, Cillia," one of the men said. "The rain is making our job harder."

"That's no excuse," Ms. Spark snapped.

"You were hired to do a job in a certain length of time."

The men moved toward the back of the house. I saw them stop in the hallway and talk. The one who had mentioned the weather kept looking at Ms. Spark.

"Hi, girls. I certainly can count on you to be here and work hard, can't I?" Ms. Spark said. "Now who's this?"

"This is Jessi Ramsey," I said. "Jessi, this is Ms. Spark."

"I'm really excited about having a new bookstore in town," said Jessi.

"You may be one of the few," replied Ms. Spark. Jessi and Mal glanced my way. Like me, they must have heard echoes of our BSC discussion in what she said. "Why don't you come help me with the new books?" she said to Jessi.

"Mary Anne, there are some things on the shelves in Benson Dalton Gable's office that need to be boxed up. Would you mind?"

"And I'll baby-sit for Tom and Gillian," offered Mal.

"They're upstairs," said Ms. Spark. Mal headed that way.

Ms. Spark led Jessi to the receiving room and I went into the small office. Two men were working to replace the drywall they'd had to remove the day before.

"Hi, Mary Anne. Cillia said you would need some boxes," said Mr. Cates, setting a few empties inside the door to the office.

"Thanks." I knelt on the floor and started pulling the old books off the lowest shelf and packing them into a box.

"What does he think he's doing, anyway?" I heard one of the workmen say. "Does this town really need another bookstore?"

"I thought they were going to tear this place down and build some new houses," said the other.

"It would have been a lot easier to do that than to redo this place," the first man answered.

I felt strange eavesdropping. Maybe they didn't realize I was still there. I cleared my throat. "Excuse me," I said. (It's hard for me to talk to people I don't know.)

"Hi. Didn't know you were still there," said the man who had helped Mr. Cates with the drywall.

"I was wondering if anybody ever found a leak in the water pipes? I heard something when I was here on Saturday and told Mr. Cates about it," I said. "It didn't sound like a drip, but . . ."

The man sighed loudly. "I guess I'd better check. Cates never said anything about a leak. I tell you, old houses are more trouble than they're worth." He stomped out. "When is Cates going to figure that out?" I heard him mumble as he went down the hall.

This little conversation gave me something else to think about. How far would these guys be willing to go to stop the opening of the bookstore? Tearing the Gable house down and building new houses would mean steady work and a lot of money for them. I decided to add them to the list of suspects in the mystery notebook.

As I removed another section of books, I felt some ridges on the bottom of the shelf. I ran my fingers over them. I scooted closer. I couldn't stifle a gasp when I read what was carved into the shelf.

"What's the matter?" asked the man still working on the wall.

"There's something, a word, carved in the wood here," I said. It was as if someone had pressed down hard and made the impression of the word in handwriting, then carved it deeper. The writing was old-style cursive — Edgar Allan Poe old.

"That shelf has been here forever. Some kid probably did it when his mom wasn't looking."

How many kids used the word *nevermore*? The one place I'd seen the word recently was in an Edgar Allan Poe poem, "The Raven." Alex had claimed that Poe's inspiration for the poem came from the ravens carved in the fireplace mantel. Had Poe carved the word into the shelf? I wanted to show it to Mr. Cates.

"Sorry to bother you again," I said, sticking my head inside the open door to Mr. Cates's office. "But I want to show you something. I found the word *nevermore* carved on one of the bookshelves."

"Let me find Cillia," he said, standing up.

I finished clearing the shelf while he went in search of Ms. Spark. When they came into the room, I moved out of the way. Ms. Spark looked at the carving, then began to quote, " 'Once upon a midnight dreary, while I pondered, weak and weary,/Over many a quaint and curious volume of forgotten lore . . .' "

" 'vainly I had sought to borrow/From my surcease of sorrow,' " Mr. Cates continued.

Together they said, " 'Quoth the Raven "Nevermore." ' "

It was only bits and pieces of the poem, but they knew the words by heart.

"This is wasted back here," said Ms. Spark. "You should move it into the front room where the customers can see it. Authentic Edgar Allan Poe graffiti."

"If that's what it is," said Mr. Cates. "Anybody could have written it."

"But Poe was here. The ravens are here," said Ms. Spark.

Hopefully, the body isn't here, I thought.

"I'll move it anyway," said Mr. Cates. "You can't have too many bookshelves in a bookstore. Come tell me when you're finished," he said to me.

Sure enough, when I was done I found Mr. Cates hard at work at his desk.

"Let's see how you did," he said. When he stepped away from the desk, a piece of paper floated behind him.

I leaned down to pick it up. It was a note. Two words caught my eye: "Annabel Lee." Here was something else that pointed to Edgar Allan Poe! A note signed by a character Poe created.

"Mr. Cates! You dropped this." I handed it to him.

Mr. Cates looked at the note, then flushed a deep brick-red. "Don't mention you saw this to Cillia, okay?" he said to me as he stuffed it into his pocket.

"I won't," I promised. But I wondered what it meant.

CHAPTER 8

"Do you know what you're going to do for your assignment?" Ms. Belcher asked me. I'd stayed after school to talk to her about my project — and about Professor Kingsolver.

"I have a couple of ideas, but I wanted to talk to you."

"Go ahead."

"I've been working at the Gable house."

"Benson Dalton Gable's house?" said Ms. Belcher, looking surprised.

"It's being turned into a bookstore, a mystery bookstore, called Poe and Co.," I told her.

"I think I read about that in the paper. Fits right in," murmured Ms. Belcher.

"With my project?" I asked.

"With that, and with the rumors about Poe having visited Gable there," she said.

"I wondered if I could work that into my project."

"What did you have in mind?"

"I'm not sure. I thought about writing a story set in the house, with Poe and Gable as characters. I also thought about making a diorama of Benson Dalton Gable's office and putting him and Poe in it," I explained. "Or maybe making up a series of letters between them."

"Sounds interesting," Ms. Belcher said, but she was looking out the window and drumming her fingers on her desk.

"But? You don't sound very sure about it."

"I took a course at Stoneybrook University with Professor Kingsolver, the woman who spoke to your class. She spent an entire session talking about Poe's visits to Gable," said Ms. Belcher.

"I've seen her at Poe and Co. a couple of times," I told Ms. Belcher.

"Aha! So she's convinced you that there's something to her theory?"

"I think it's interesting that they may have had some kind of relationship, Poe and Gable," I said.

"But do you think Poe might have had an argument with Gable over a manuscript and killed him? No one has found a Poe manuscript there, have they?"

I took in a quick breath. This was the most direct expression I'd heard yet that Poe might have killed Gable. Of course, Alex had hinted at it. "No manuscripts, and I don't know about any murder," I admitted. "It's an interesting idea, and the house is weird — spooky, strange noises, odd happenings that could make you think the place is . . ."

"Haunted?" asked Ms. Belcher.

"Yes," I answered.

"What an excellent site for a mystery bookstore!" Ms. Belcher said. "When does it open? I'd like to meet the ghost." She smiled.

"Soon," I replied. "The rain has slowed some of the work." I didn't think I needed to be any more specific.

"I'd think about a combination of your ideas. You know what the house looks like, and it would be interesting to see you reproduce it in a diorama. However, I'd also like the project to have a written component. Perhaps the letters? I'm certain Professor Kingsolver would be happy to talk with you."

"Okay. Thanks," I said. "See you tomorrow."

I splashed my way to the bookstore, thinking about my project. I decided to set my diorama in the office with the big desk and place Poe on one side and Gable on the other. I'd show manuscript pages spread between them, and a bookcase with *nevermore* carved on one of the shelves. The letters would be the hard part of the project. What would Poe and Gable write to one another?

Only three cars were parked outside the store when I arrived. I opened the door. The store was unusually quiet. No one yelling, no hammering, nothing.

"Anybody here?" I called out.

"We're in my office," Mr. Cates called.

I hung up my raincoat and headed for the office. "Hi. Where is everybody?" I asked. Then I noticed that Mr. Cates and Ms. Spark weren't alone. Professor Kingsolver was sitting in a chair beside Ms. Spark.

Mr. Cates cleared his throat. "I sent the kids off with Kristy because of . . . what happened here this afternoon. Besides, they're very tired of hanging around here all the time."

"What happened?" I asked.

He cleared his throat again, looked at the blotter on his desk, then looked back at me. "One of the workmen thinks he saw a ghost in the basement."

"A ghost!" I clutched the edge of the desk. The house *was* haunted.

"Andy, the foreman, was in the basement working on the electrical wiring when he heard a noise, a rustling. He thought maybe it was a mouse or Pluto, but when he turned around, he saw a grayish shadowy shape behind him. It kept moving and shifting. He said he thought 'ghost' right away, but he knew that was silly. Instead, he decided the other men were playing a joke on him.

"He ran upstairs. Everybody on the crew

was moving bookshelves around. They all claimed they didn't know anything about it."

"It's Benson Dalton Gable, trying to tell you his secrets," said Professor Kingsolver breathlessly.

"Ramona, you're being a little dramatic," Ms. Spark said.

"What secrets? That Edgar Allan Poe killed him?" I asked.

"Where did you hear a thing like that?" Professor Kingsolver demanded.

"From Alex Gable, and from my English teacher, Ms. Belcher. Alex said that Gable died soon after a visit from Poe, and that the family doesn't know where the body is buried. Ms. Belcher said that Poe may have murdered him in a disagreement over a manuscript. At least, she said that's what you told your class."

"I did say that." Professor Kingsolver pressed her knuckles against her mouth. "I hope we haven't bestirred evil best left at rest."

"At least we know where Gable's buried now," Mr. Cates said.

I turned sharply. "What do you mean?"

"Come with us. I was about to show Professor Kingsolver. You can see it too." Mr. Cates beckoned for me to follow.

I followed the grown-ups, looking behind

me every few steps. Thunder rumbled when Mr. Cates opened the door to the basement.

At the top of the stairs, everyone paused. I heard someone take a deep breath. I did the same thing.

The steps creaked as we descended. I kept feeling a cold breath of air tickling the back of my neck. The air cooled with each step down.

The door slammed closed behind us. It startled me so that I had to clutch the stair rail to keep from falling.

"Just the wind catching the door," Mr. Cates said. His voice sounded unnaturally loud in the silence of the basement.

Then the light flickered. Mr. Cates, Ms. Spark, and Professor Kingsolver waited for me at the bottom of the steps. With one last look over my shoulder, I joined them.

"After the work crew denied any knowledge of the 'ghost,' Andy went back downstairs and looked around to see how a ghost might have been rigged up. He moved some stuff around and found this." Mr. Cates pointed at a gray slab that stood out from the rest of the stone floor.

I leaned closer and read, " 'To-day I wear these chains, and am *here*. To-morrow I shall be fetterless — but *where*?' "

"Poe again," whispered Professor Kingsolver.

"Do you think Mr. Gable is . . ." I pointed at the slab.

"An old boiler used to sit on top of it. And it looks like a tombstone," said Mr. Cates. "I'm sure we could find out, but I don't know whether I want to. For one thing, you need all kinds of permits to dig up a grave and I don't want anything more to delay the opening of the store."

"So you're just going to leave it down here?" I asked.

"For now," said Ms. Spark.

I shivered again. Poor Tom and Gillian! To live in a house with a grave in the basement — I didn't even want to think about the kind of nightmares I might have.

"Mr. Cates! Are you here?" A woman's voice drifted down from upstairs.

"Who's that?" Ms. Sparks asked.

Annabel Lee was my first thought, but I didn't say anything.

Mr. Cates, Ms. Spark, and Professor King-solver headed for the stairs and I hurried after them.

"Mr. Cates! Hi, I'm Kim Simon from the *Stoneybrook News*. We had an appointment to talk about the opening of your store." A woman of medium height, with short hair and glasses, waited in the front room of the store. A big canvas bag was slung over her shoulder.

"That's right. In all the excitement, I'd forgotten. It's nice to meet you," said Mr. Cates.

"I think I'll run along," said Professor Kingsolver, "but you've certainly given me much food for thought. I'll talk to you about it after I do some research."

"What with the ghost and the grave and everything else, it's no wonder we forgot," said Ms. Spark.

Ms. Simon looked up.

"Cillia," said Mr. Cates, a note of warning in his voice. Then, to the reporter, he said, "This is Cillia Spark. She's a bookstore designer. And this is Mary Anne Spier, who is helping us prepare for the opening. Sometimes she baby-sits, sometimes she packs boxes. . . ."

"And sometimes she hears strange heartbeats," Ms. Spark added.

"Aren't you one of the members of the Baby-sitters Club?" Ms. Simon asked. I nodded. "I've heard about you guys. You've solved some mysteries here in Stoneybrook, haven't you?"

I nodded again.

"Mysteries? You didn't mention that, Mary Anne," Ms. Spark said.

"It never came up," I answered. My cheeks felt hot and I knew I was turning red.

"Our own Dupin," said Mr. Cates.

"What was that you said about a ghost and a grave?" Ms. Simon turned the conversation back to the store.

"We had quite an interesting occurrence here today," said Ms. Spark. She explained about the workman seeing the "ghost" and finding the grave.

"Could I see it? Maybe take a picture?" Ms. Simon asked.

"It's too silly," said Mr. Cates. "That's not what I want people to think about when they hear Poe and Co."

"It would give me an interesting angle for the story," said Ms. Simon.

"Maybe we should tell her about the bookshelf and finding the cat trapped behind the wall," said Ms. Spark, in a low but audible voice.

Mr. Cates shook his head and frowned at Ms. Spark.

"What?" Ms. Simon asked.

"There have been several interesting . . . occurrences since we started working on the store," said Mr. Cates. "But I'd like to talk about some things we have planned for the *future*."

"One of the things I'd like to know more about is Edgar Allan Poe's connection to the house," said Ms. Simon.

"Then you'd definitely be interested in the,"

Ms. Spark paused, glancing at Mr. Cates, "occurrences. They all have a Poe connection."

Ms. Simon turned away from Mr. Cates. "Tell me about the occurrences."

Since I was supposed to be working, I thought I should find something to do. Papers were scattered all over the counter. I could straighten them while I listened.

"One night Mary Anne, our Dupin, was waiting for a delivery, and she heard the beating of a heart. Now, there's a Poe story called 'The Tell-Tale Heart,' " began Ms. Spark.

"I know it well," said Ms. Simon, writing in her notebook.

Mr. Cates leaned against the wall and watched as Ms. Spark talked to the reporter.

"Then we discovered the word *nevermore* carved into one of the shelves of this bookcase," said Ms. Spark, walking to the case and pointing at the carving.

" 'The Raven,' " said Ms. Simon.

"And this fireplace mantel has a raven motif," said Ms. Spark, gesturing toward it. "It was original. We didn't add it. One of Gable's descendants claims that this is what inspired Poe's poem."

"Or did he steal the poem from Gable?" Ms. Simon asked.

"No one ever accused him of stealing anything," said Mr. Cates.

"But I've heard the rumors," said Ms. Simon. "Also a rumor that he killed Mr. Gable because he was jealous of him, or because Gable threatened to expose him for stealing some of his writings."

"Those are all just rumors," said Ms. Spark.

"And I shall treat them as such. They're fairly well known around Stoneybrook," Ms. Simon said.

If it was all so well known, why hadn't I heard about any of it until now?

"And don't forget about Pluto," said Ms. Spark.

"Pluto, as in 'The Black Cat'?" asked Ms. Simon.

"You know your Poe!" said Ms. Spark.

"I did a little research for the article," said Ms. Simon.

"Anyway, one day Mary Anne was in Benson Dalton Gable's office, and she heard a cat behind the wall. It was Pluto. He'd crawled back there when the old walls were ripped out and didn't crawl out before the new walls were nailed in place."

"Great stuff!" said Ms. Simon. "Let me take a few pictures and I'll have a dynamite story here."

Ms. Simon insisted that I be in the picture with the bookshelf, since I'd discovered the word *nevermore*. When she was finished taking photographs, Mr. Cates said I might as well go home. We weren't going to accomplish anything that day anyway. It was almost time for the BSC meeting, so I headed straight for Claudia's.

CHAPTER 9

Wednesday

I really had my hands full today. I brought Tom and Gillian to my house. David Michael, Andrew, and Karen were already there. I needed major baby-sitting help, so Aunt Cecilia brought over Jessi with Becca in tow. Together, we may have come up with an antidote to the rainy-day blues. And I definitely found out part of what makes Tom and Gillian act the way they do. I don't know if I was any help, but maybe.

"Kristy, can we please play some softball?" asked Karen. "I want to be good this season and I need practice."

"We all need practice to work out the winter kinks, but there's no way we can play inside," Kristy replied, rolling her softball under the sofa.

"But it's a softball," said David Michael. "Why can't we practice grounders at least?"

"Not inside," Kristy said again, looking at Jessi.

"Let's . . . read a book. What would you like to hear, Gillian?" Jessi asked.

The kids groaned.

"All we've done for the last million years is read books," said Becca.

Tom and Gillian sat side by side on the sofa. Tom looked everyplace but at the rest of the kids.

"Shall we play a game?" offered Kristy. "Suggestions welcome."

"Tennis," said Becca.

"That's an outside game," Kristy said. "I was thinking of a board game."

The kids groaned again.

"Just let us watch TV," said David Michael.

"No way," said Kristy.

"We could race," said Karen. "We could have

different kinds of races, like a crawling race or a worm race or a relay race."

Kristy thought for a minute. "Races could be inside activities. Let's start with a crawling race, okay?"

"Line up over here," Jessi said, taking a position at one side of the room.

Kristy moved some of the furniture out of the way. Tom and Gillian remained on the couch.

"Come on, guys. Line up with the rest of the kids," she said to them.

"No way," said Tom.

"Gillian?" said Kristy.

Gillian looked at Tom, hesitated for a moment, then scooted off the couch and took a place at the end of the row.

"This will be a crawling race, on your hands and knees," Kristy explained. "Jessi will give you the signal to go, then I'll be here at the finish line to see who wins. And my decision is final."

"Everybody down, get set, GO!" Jessi said.

The kids shot off. Soon Andrew was ahead. David Michael moved at a steady angle, into Karen's path.

"David Michael! You are in my way. Did Andrew tell you to do that so he could win? You are cheating!" she said.

"I am not cheating. I was trying to go straight," David Michael protested.

"Andrew is the winner!" Kristy proclaimed.

"Only because he cheated," Karen mumbled.

"I did not cheat. You were not even close to me," said Andrew.

"I would have been if David Michael hadn't blocked my way. I was starting to catch up when he ran into me," said Karen.

"Andrew is the winner," Kristy repeated.

"I don't want to race anymore," said Karen.

"I have another idea," said Kristy. "What about hide-and-seek?"

"Andrew has to be 'it,' since he cheated to win the race," said Karen.

"I don't mind," said Andrew.

"Tom, come play this time," said Kristy.

"Can we hide anyplace at all in this big house?" Tom asked.

"Stay on the first floor," said Kristy.

Andrew covered his eyes and started counting. The kids spread out. "Ready or not, here I come!" Andrew yelled.

He ran to the closet in the hall and opened the door. Becca popped out, giggling, and raced him to home base on the sofa, but Andrew tagged her first. Then David Michael crawled out from under a table and dashed for base, but Andrew tagged him too.

Kristy saw Karen crawling toward the sofa from behind the kitchen door.

"I see you!" Andrew yelled, tripping on the

rug trying to reach her. This set off a storm of giggles from the girls.

"Free!" Karen yelled, touching home base.

"Two more," said Kristy.

Andrew wandered into the living room, the dining room, and through to the kitchen. "I don't see them," he said.

"Look harder," said Jessi.

Tom and Gillian popped out from behind the television when Andrew started out the door the second time. Andrew turned and dived for the sofa.

"Tie!" said Kristy.

"What is going on in here?" Watson Brewer asked, coming as far as the door and no farther.

"Hide-and-seek," said Kristy.

"Come play with us, Daddy," said Karen. "You can be 'it.' "

"I'd like to, but I'm working," Watson said.

"Please, Daddy," said Andrew.

He shook his head.

"Sorry we were so loud, Watson," said Kristy.

"That's okay. It sounded like a party out here, and I needed a break." Watson turned and left.

"A party," said Kristy. "That's what we need to pull us out of this slump. A festival would be even better — a Rainy Day Festival."

"I'd rather have a Sunny Day Festival," said Karen.

"We'll have sunny-day activities," said Kristy. "Who can think of some?"

"Everybody has to wear sunglasses," Jessi suggested.

"Good idea," said Kristy. She scrambled to find a piece of paper and a pencil. "We can have it this Saturday in our garage. We can do outside stuff in there if the weather is still bad, and not have to worry about the noise and everything."

"Sand castles," said Gillian softly.

"Great idea! We could use sand from Emily Michelle's sandbox. That's a great sunny-day activity." Kristy added it to the list.

"Rainbows," said Becca. "We could paint rainbows."

"Maybe use colored chalk," Jessi suggested.

"Let's have a parade," said Andrew.

"And dances," said Karen.

"Games," put in David Michael.

"These are great ideas!" Kristy said. "You guys need to make invitations for everybody. We can make them in the shape of sunbursts. Let me find the art supplies. Do you know where they are, Karen?"

"I will go look," she offered.

"Is anyone hungry?" Kristy asked. "I could

make a snack while we're waiting for Karen to find the art supplies."

"I'll help you," said Tom.

"Thanks," replied Kristy. In the kitchen she found a stack of paper cups and handed Tom a bottle of juice.

"Who was that man who came in awhile ago?" Tom asked.

"That's Watson. He's Karen and Andrew's dad, and he's married to my mom, so he's my stepfather." Kristy found some cookies and napkins. "My dad left us when David Michael was a baby."

Tom looked up, and juice overflowed the cup he was filling.

Kristy used a napkin to wipe up the spill.

"What did your mom do to make him leave?" Tom asked.

"She didn't make him leave."

"What did you do? Or David Michael?"

"We didn't do anything either. No one made him leave. He decided he didn't want to be here anymore and he just left."

Tom poured the juice more carefully now. "Does he write you letters? How often does he come visit?"

"Not very often," Kristy said. "And sometimes I'm mad at him for not being here. I think he still loves us, but I also think he's missing out on a lot. We have our mom, though, and now

Watson, so we're pretty lucky. But it's hard."

"Yeah," said Tom softly. "You know what? Sometimes I think my dad married my mom just because her name is Annabel Lee. He likes Edgar Allan Poe a lot."

"Your mom's name is Annabel Lee?" Kristy asked.

"She doesn't like it much," said Tom. "But she'd be perfect in the bookstore now, with that name. Except, I think my dad likes Ms. Spark. And if he does, Mom may never come back."

"Ms. Spark is pretty nice, and she and your dad have a lot in common. It won't be her fault if your mom doesn't come back," Kristy tried to explain.

"It's so hard," Tom said.

Kristy told me later that she thought he sounded as if he wanted to cry.

"Hey," Kristy said, "whenever you have questions about any of this stuff, you can ask me. I'm the resident expert on parents who leave."

Tom actually smiled at Kristy then.

"I think Tom finally felt as if he and Gillian weren't the only kids in the whole world whose mom or dad has left," Kristy said at the BSC meeting.

"And for the rest of the afternoon he was much more pleasant," added Jessi.

"Annabel Lee is his mother's name? Then the note I found must have been from her," I said.

"What note?" asked Kristy.

"I found a note on the floor signed Annabel Lee, and I gave it to Mr. Cates. He asked me not to mention it to Ms. Spark. I guess because it was from his wife."

Our conversation returned to the festival, and I tried to concentrate on the plans, but I kept imagining everyone's response when I told them about the ghost.

"Maybe the festival is what we need to make the sun come out," said Mal.

"The kids were excited about the idea," said Kristy, "and once we started making invitations, they didn't fight once."

"Then it was worth it," said Mal.

"Who worked at the Gable house today?" asked Jessi.

My cue, finally. "I did," I said. "But I didn't actually work. Things came pretty much to a standstill after one of the workmen saw a ghost in the basement. At least, he thought he saw a ghost."

"What!" said Stacey.

"I can't believe it," said Claudia.

"I *thought* the house was haunted," said Abby.

"Why didn't you tell us first thing?" Kristy asked.

"You were already discussing the festival and — "

"Tell us now," Stacey insisted.

"That's one reason Mr. Cates asked you to take the kids out of the store," I said to Kristy.

"I thought it was for more than a change of scene. Mr. Cates looked kind of shaky when I came by," Kristy said.

"Anyway, when the workman looked around to see where the ghost had come from — he thought it was a joke — he found a slab of rock with an inscription carved on it, and the words are from Poe. Mr. Cates thinks it might be Benson Dalton Gable's grave," I said slowly.

My friends shrieked.

"That's gross," said Mal.

"Scary," said Stacey, a smile playing around the corners of her lips.

"Things are a little tense over there. Mr. Cates is worried that when the store finally opens, no one will come because of the ghost."

"How will they know?" asked Mal.

"A reporter from the *Stoneybrook News* came by to write a story about the bookstore. Ms. Spark mentioned the ghost — and everything else that's happened so far too. So the reporter's going to write about that instead," I went on.

"I was beginning to think, after talking to Tom, that he and Gillian had come up with all these things to scare off Ms. Spark. But I doubt Tom and Gillian could create a ghost, or plant a tombstone, without some help," said Kristy.

"If they aren't the real things," said Stacey.

"Professor Kingsolver was also at the store this afternoon," I said. "Did you find out anything else about her?" I asked Claudia.

"Janine said she doesn't know her because she teaches English, not math or science," Claudia replied.

"I talked to Ms. Belcher about her. She says that Professor Kingsolver thinks Poe might have murdered Gable over a manuscript," I said. Everyone had moved into a tight little circle by now.

"Alex said sort of the same thing," said Stacey. "Remember? He didn't come right out with it, but he hinted that Poe might have had something to do with Gable's death."

"And I asked my brothers about Alex Gable," said Kristy. "Charlie said he went to a Halloween party at the Gable house once, and it was scary then too. He also said that he'd heard Alex say he planned to fix up the house someday and live in it. He wanted to turn it into a little museum or something, dedicated to Benson Dalton Gable."

"So Alex can't have been too happy when his father sold the place," I said.

"I guess not," said Kristy. "But the question is whether he's unhappy enough to try to run off the new owners."

"Professor Kingsolver is so superstitious, she doesn't really seem like the type to come up with a scheme like this either," said Mal. "I can't imagine her even *touching* a black cat. But she *does* keep coming around."

"The construction workers are unhappy too," I said. "I overheard one of them say that he wishes they'd torn the house down and built new ones in its place. Come to think of it, it was the same guy who saw the ghost *and* who put up the drywall, trapping Pluto.

"I wish Dawn were here. She loves ghosts and ghostly things," I said.

"Do you think it could be a *real* ghost?" asked Abby.

"That's one of the things we need to find out," Kristy replied.

"If Benson Dalton Gable is buried in the basement, it *could* be a real ghost," Mal said in a very quiet voice.

"Especially if he was murdered," Jessi added.

I wasn't the only who shivered at their words.

"Let's investigate all the *people* who might be

behind the mystery before we start believing in ghosts," Kristy said.

"I'll keep an eye on Ms. Spark. She has some interesting ideas about design and I'm having a good time working with her anyway," said Claudia.

"And one or another of us will be spending time with Tom and Gillian," said Abby.

"I think I'll look at the Poe stories again," I said.

"I'd like to see the tombstone," Stacey said. "And maybe meet Benson Dalton Gable."

We laughed a little nervously.

CHAPTER 10

"Kristy!" Tom was waiting at the door when Kristy, Logan, Claudia, and I arrived at Poe and Co. on Thursday. He didn't even look at the rest of us. "Gillian and I have another idea for the Sunny Day Festival. We thought you could work on it with us . . . if you want," he added.

"That would be great," Kristy agreed. "Did you give any invitations to kids in your class?"

Tom nodded. "And I ate lunch with Byron Pike so we could talk about this idea I have."

"Let's go upstairs, out of the way, and talk about it some more," said Kristy.

Going upstairs to talk was a good idea. The noise level was so high in the front room that it was almost impossible to hear anything. The room seemed filled with workmen, and each one was doing something noisy. The walls were finally lined with fixed shelves, and Ms. Spark was showing the men where to place the free-standing bookcases. Two men were hooking up a computer at the checkout desk and several other workers were on ladders, installing lighting in the ceiling.

We were still standing in the doorway, waiting for some men carrying a shelf to pass, when Alex Gable opened the outside door and pushed in beside us.

"Good picture," he said to me, holding up that day's edition of the *Stoneybrook News*. I'd spent most of the day listening to comments about the picture and answering questions about the ghost at Poe and Co.

"I told Mom to buy extra copies," said Logan.

"It's Dupin," Ms. Spark said, putting her arm around me and pulling me close. She'd finished telling the men where to move the shelves and joined us. "Did you see the story in the paper?" she asked. Her eyes were brighter and her smile bigger than ever.

I made myself smile. She couldn't realize how many times I'd heard those words today.

"So, Dupin," said Alex, teasing, "have you solved the mystery of what happened to my long-lost ancestor yet?"

"We may have to call in Nancy Drew," Claudia said.

"And the Hardy Boys," Logan added.

"You guys are probably every bit as good as

they are," said Ms. Spark. "What do you think about all the work that's finally being done?"

"Pretty amazing," I said. "Do you still need us?"

"Of course we do!"

"I'd like to see the stone in the basement," said Alex. "Mary Anne, maybe you could show it to me?"

I shook my head. I wasn't at all anxious to go down there again.

"You may have noticed that no one is in the basement today," said Ms. Spark. "Larry isn't supposed to let anyone go down there until the police have finished looking at the area. Someone from the county will investigate when they find the time."

"Dupin, it seems you have your work cut out for you," said Alex. "You, of course, know that observation is the key."

I also knew that Alex was speaking about Dupin's technique in the stories Poe wrote featuring the detective.

"Yet you have to do more than simply observe," he continued. "You must know *what* to observe, and remember to look at the matter as a whole and not as a series of parts."

"You've been doing your homework," said Ms. Spark.

I looked around the room again, *observing* the activity. Alex may have been pulling my leg, but he was right. I had to remember to look at things as a whole. It was easy to start looking at each incident individually and not consider the bigger picture.

Why was *Alex* teasing me about solving the mystery anyway? Did he think I couldn't figure it out without his help? Or was he trying to show us how clever he is? Maybe he wanted to feel a part of Poe and Co., I finally decided as I watched him wander around the room looking at the changes.

Ms. Spark pulled me back to the matter at hand. "I've already set aside some jobs for you," she said. "Larry is tied up answering the phone — everybody's calling to find out when the store is going to open. It doesn't seem as if the possibility of a ghost is going to deter customers one bit. Anyway, we want to be able to take advantage of all the interest and open as soon as possible," Ms. Spark continued.

"I'd like to finish the designs I started," said Claudia, "unless you have something else for me to do."

"I was hoping you'd help me with an announcement we want to send out to potential customers," said Ms. Spark. "I have the wording, but it needs an illustration."

"Tell me what you want and I'll see if I can do it," said Claudia.

"Great. Logan, want to do a little more painting? The walls are up in the kitchen and they need a coat of primer."

"I'll go start." Logan took off for the back of the store.

"And Mary Anne, there's a stack of envelopes and mailing labels in Benson Dalton Gable's office. Would you mind putting a label on each envelope? It's boring, I know, but it's one of those things that has to be done. When I started working in Hollywood all I did was check props off a list. That was my entire job, but it led to better opportunities," said Ms. Spark.

"You worked in Hollywood?" exclaimed Claudia.

"I was a set designer. My husband — my *ex*-husband — was in special effects. It was fun for awhile," said Ms. Spark. "And designing a theme for a bookstore is similar to set design."

"I'd like to stick around and help too, if that's okay," Alex offered.

"Sure. We'll take all the help we can get." Ms. Spark looked around as if trying to find him a job.

"I'll keep Mary Anne company," said Alex.

I didn't know why he wanted to help stick labels on envelopes, but if he stayed around maybe I could find out more about Gable. And Alex.

"Hi," said Professor Kingsolver, opening the

front door and sticking her head inside. "Is the cat nearby?"

"I think Pluto is upstairs with Tom and Gillian," said Ms. Spark.

Professor Kingsolver stepped inside. "What wonderful coverage you received in the news. I've been trying to call, but the phone has been busy all day."

"Constant calls," said Ms. Spark.

"The newspaper doesn't say whether Mr. Cates plans to exhume the grave."

"We don't even know if it is a grave. The police have asked us to do nothing for the time being. Besides, we're trying to open a bookstore."

"Is Mr. Cates here? I have this book I promised to drop by," said Professor Kingsolver.

"I'll give the book to Larry," said Ms. Spark.

"No, there are a few things I'd like to point out," said Professor Kingsolver, clutching the book to her chest. "You know, this is finally looking like a bookstore!"

That put the sparkle back in Ms. Spark. "It does, doesn't it? A lot of the credit goes to Andy and his crew." Ms. Spark smiled at the construction foreman, who was standing behind her.

"I didn't think the old place could look this

good," the foreman admitted. "I'll be glad, though, when this job is finished."

Tom and Gillian burst into the room, with Kristy following more slowly. "Where's Dad?" Tom asked.

"In the office, answering the phone," said Ms. Spark. "Maybe I can help you."

"We're looking for the stereo. I thought it was in a box in Dad's bedroom, but we can't find it," said Tom.

"It must be in a box someplace," said Ms. Spark. "If you don't find it upstairs, come back. I'll mention it to your dad in the meantime."

"Please don't forget," said Tom.

"I won't."

Kristy and I exchanged looks. Tom was actually being civil to Ms. Spark.

"And maybe Kristy can help you write reviews on those cards I had made up for the children's section," said Ms. Spark. "Remember when you suggested that we post reviews of some of the books for the customers?" she asked Kristy. "Tom and Gillian have some favorites too. I thought it would be appropriate to let them start the project."

"Good idea," said Kristy. "I'd love to help. We can listen to music while we do it."

"If we ever find the stereo," said Gillian.

"I may have a tape player in my car," said

Ms. Spark. "If you don't find the stereo, we'll work out something." She pushed Gillian's bangs out of her eyes and Gillian smiled at her.

The kids and Ms. Spark seemed to be getting along a lot better. If the "hauntings" were part of Tom and Gillian's plan to scare Ms. Spark away, they might stop now, I thought.

Suddenly, I heard a strange noise, a rustling from the hallway. I turned — just in time to see a huge black bird swoop out of the darkness. I covered my head with my arms. Hammers clattered to the floor and even the grown men ducked. Professor Kingsolver shrieked and pressed herself against the wall.

Kristy gathered Tom and Gillian close to her.

When I finally looked up again, the bird was perched on a small bust of Edgar Allan Poe that stood on the fireplace mantel. Its black eyes darted from one corner of the room to the other. Ms. Spark was staring at the bird, her mouth open. Alex had covered his head with the newspaper.

"What in the world is going on in here?" Mr. Cates asked, standing in the doorway the bird had come through a moment before.

"It's . . . it's a raven," Ms. Spark said in little more than a whisper, although I wasn't sure that was so.

"I'll take care of it," said Andy.

"No!" Ms. Spark placed her hand on his arm.

The bird continued to sit calmly, looking at each one of us, I thought.

In the background, I could hear the workmen talking quietly to one another.

"Where's Pluto?" Kristy asked. "All we need now is for him to come in and chase the bird."

"You go upstairs and make sure he stays away," said Ms. Spark.

Kristy kept Tom and Gillian close to her as they left to find the cat.

"We certainly wouldn't want anything to happen to Lenore," Alex said, the newspaper still on his head.

Was the raven in Edgar Allan Poe's poem named Lenore? I remembered the name from something I'd read recently — and I'd read a lot of Poe, including "The Raven."

"I may have a cage around here someplace," said Mr. Cates. "Let me see if I can find it and lure the bird inside. Someone is missing a pet, I'll bet."

"I wish Ms. Simon were here now," said Ms. Spark. "This would make a terrific picture. In fact, I'm going to find my camera." She followed Mr. Cates down the hall.

Logan joined Claudia and me.

"Did the bird come in through the kitchen?" I asked him.

"I don't think so. And I would have noticed that."

"I need to go," said Professor Kingsolver, fumbling with the doorknob. "I can't stay in the same room with a bird. I'm allergic." She sniffed. I noticed her eyes were red-rimmed as she slipped out into the rain.

"She's very emotional, isn't she?" said Claudia.

"Edgar Allan Poe strikes again, right, Dupin?" said Alex, finally lowering the newspaper.

Mr. Cates returned, swinging a large birdcage. Lenore (I couldn't think of the raven any other way, thanks to Alex) remained on the bust.

"Let me take a picture first," said Ms. Spark.

Mr. Cates moved out of the way, and the camera clicked and whirred.

"That's what I'll draw on the invitations," said Claudia. "A raven."

"Appropriate," said Alex.

"Are you okay?" Logan moved a little closer to me.

"Fine," I answered. "Ready to work." As far as work went, I had more in mind than sticking labels on envelopes. For instance, figuring out how Lenore found her way inside this particular house.

Mr. Cates managed to trap the raven inside the cage, which he then carried to his office.

"Where did it come from?" I asked Logan as

we walked down the hall. Almost in answer to my question I felt a draft — from Benson Dalton Gable's study. I stepped into the room and saw that the window was open.

"I guess it flew in there," said Logan. "And since it does seem to be a pet, I can't blame it for wanting to come in out of the rain."

"But a raven finding its way to a bookstore called Poe and Co.? It seems a little more than coincidence. Especially when you add it to the sound of the beating heart we heard and the other things I haven't had time to tell you about." I stuck my head out the window and observed the ground underneath. It was so wet that any footprints would have vanished immediately.

"Everybody except Mr. Cates and me was in the room with you when the raven flew in," Logan pointed out.

"I know, but someone could have released the bird a few minutes earlier."

"Check shoes," suggested Logan. "Anybody who was outside this window will have mud caked on their shoes."

"Professor Kingsolver left," I said, "but she said she was allergic and her eyes were turning red. I'd better hurry before Alex leaves too."

In the hall I met Mr. Cates. "Lenore is a good name for the bird, don't you think?" he asked. "I wonder what Lenore eats."

"Birdseed?" I answered.

"I guess I'll have to go buy some," Mr. Cates said.

I tried not to be too obvious as I looked at Mr. Cates's shoes. He was wearing running shoes, white ones, and there wasn't any more mud on them than I'd expect.

Upstairs, Kristy, Tom, and Gillian were hard at work, writing mini-reviews for their favorite books. The kids were wearing socks.

"Did you find Pluto?" I asked. "The bird is in a cage, so Pluto doesn't have to stay up here."

"He's asleep," said Gillian, "on the couch."

And he was, looking like a round, furry black pillow, curled up in the corner of the couch.

"Where are your shoes?" I asked.

"Over there," said Gillian. "We don't like to wear them when we're home. Dad makes us wear them downstairs because of all the nails, but as soon as we come up here, they're off."

Four shoes were piled inside the door. Again, there didn't seem to be unusual amounts of mud on them.

Downstairs, Alex was talking to Ms. Spark as Claudia sketched the Edgar Allan Poe bust. He could start labeling the envelopes without me, I thought. Alex also wore white running shoes with only a thin line of mud along the edges. I felt a flutter of excitement when I saw what

Ms. Spark had on her feet — blue slippers with thin rubber soles. She too must have removed her outside shoes.

"Isn't it a little risky to wear those thin slippers around all these nails?" I asked her.

Ms. Spark curled her toes inside the blue satin. "Probably," she said, "but Tom and Gillian shoenapped my oxfords and buried them in the mud. I asked them to clean the mud off, but they haven't had time yet. They'll have to do it before I leave."

So Tom and Gillian hadn't given up their old ways yet.

Andy was on a ladder, screwing a lightbulb into the fixture over the counter. His heavy work boots, and those of every other workman in the room, were mud-caked. That was no surprise, considering that their cars and trucks were parked in the lake of mud that would someday be a parking lot.

Even though looking at shoes hadn't been as helpful as I'd hoped, I reminded the Dupin in me that observation was the key to discovering the answers. I would have to keep looking.

CHAPTER 11

My new nickname made me want to know more about Poe's Dupin. I'd decided to finish reading all the stories Poe had written about him. Unfortunately, my book from school was missing "The Mystery of Marie Rogêt." I stopped by the library on Friday afternoon, on my way to Poe and Co.

After looking in the card catalog, I located *The Complete Short Stories of Edgar Allan Poe* and found the one about Marie Rogêt. As I skimmed it, I noticed that Dupin had a lot to say about newspapers and their effect on an investigation. Poe had written (in Dupin's words) that the "object of newspapers is to create a sensation rather than further the cause of truth." I thought about this for a minute. I realized that people do believe what's written in the newspaper, often without asking many questions. Yet, the information in a story is only as good as its source. For example, the story about Poe and Co. had created a sensation, if all the calls coming in yesterday were a measure of sensation. Yet the story didn't tell *why* all the things had happened at the bookstore, only *that* they had happened. Something about that bothered me, but I couldn't figure out exactly what. Maybe it would become clearer once I arrived at the store.

I checked out the book of Poe stories and stuffed it into my backpack, then rushed to the store.

As I walked through the rain I passed a pet shop. I wondered if it sold birds, big black birds. I stepped inside, setting off a buzzer. A man was stocking shelves to one side of the store. I saw brightly colored parakeets fluttering in cages in the back. In fact, they were in cages remarkably similar to the one Mr. Cates happened to have on hand for Lenore, dome-shaped and gold-colored. Of course, I didn't know how much variety there was in birdcages.

"I'll be right with you," the salesclerk said as I walked past him on my way to the birds.

All of the birds in the back of the store were parakeets, with the exception of one small yellow bird that might have been a canary. There wasn't a raven in sight.

"Now, what can I do for you?" the man asked.

"Do you sell ravens?" I asked.

He managed to look surprised and irritated at the same time, his eyes growing bigger, but frowning. "What's with the sudden interest in ravens? They aren't very attractive and they're awfully big."

"You mean you've sold someone a raven recently?"

"You're the second person to come asking that question. Not to mention the woman who bought a bird."

"Can you remember who bought it?" I asked. "And who else wanted to know about ravens?"

"It was a fellow, a young guy, who was in here asking about the birds. But I sold the bird to a woman. I didn't have one in stock. I had to arrange with another store to send me one. She wouldn't have any other kind of bird. It had to be one of those big black things," he said.

The young guy could be Alex, I thought.

"Now, why are *you* so interested in ravens?" the man asked, his eyes narrowing.

"We . . . we found one. And it seemed awfully tame, so we thought it must be a pet. I'm, um, looking for the owner."

"Uh-huh. Well, it was a cash sale, the raven. I don't have any records with the address or phone number, but I sort of remember the woman's name. It was Lenore, or something like that."

My heart almost leaped through my throat. Lenore again. Either Professor Kingsolver or Ms. Spark could have used that name. "Do you remember what the woman looked like?" I asked.

He shook his head. "Sorry," he said with a shrug. "Could I interest you in a cage or some feed?"

"No, thanks anyway. We're all set. Thanks for your help too." I started to leave.

"Hey! I could take your name. If she comes back, I could tell her you have the bird."

Quickly, I scribbled a name and number on a paper he handed me. Marie Rogêt was the name I wrote, alongside the number for Poe and Co.

When I arrived at the store, I was amazed. It actually looked like a store. The shelves were all in place, and Stacey and Mal were arranging books on them.

"I can't believe it!" I marveled, walking around the room.

"Amazing, isn't it?" said Stacey. "They plan to open Sunday, although the grand opening won't be until next Friday. You should see the invitations that Claudia came up with. There's a raven — "

"Where's Lenore?" I asked, interrupting Stacey.

"You didn't see her?" asked Mal, pointing toward the back corner of the room.

Lenore was perched in her cage, which was now hanging from a hook in the wall. Pluto was directly underneath the cage, staring at the bird.

"The cat hasn't moved since we came in,"

said Stacey. "Mr. Cates said that the newspaper reporter is going to do another story about the bird finding its way here. Then, if Lenore is somebody's pet, maybe her owners will call."

"And if nobody calls?" I asked.

"Lenore will 'join the bookstore family,' in the words of Mr. Cates," said Mal.

"Where are Ms. Spark and Mr. Cates?"

"Mr. Cates took Tom and Gillian shopping. Ms. Spark had to go to the post office to mail something."

"And are the workmen finished?" I asked.

"A couple of them are still here." Stacey looked at Mal, and they giggled. "In the basement. They're working on the wiring. Neither of them would go down alone."

"You should see them looking over their shoulders and jumping at every little sound," said Mal.

"And speaking of the basement," said Stacey, "we want to see the gravestone."

"No one is supposed to go down there," I reminded her.

"The workmen are down there now."

"Well, anyway, it may not be a 'gravestone.'"

"You're right," said Stacey. "Mal and I have been talking and we don't believe there's a dead body or a ghost behind everything that's happened."

"But we haven't come up with anything that

points to any of our suspects, either," Mal said.

"So we may as well take a look at the grave-stone, in case it will give us new information," said Stacey.

"I don't know. . . ." I could understand why they wanted to see it, but the thought of going in that cellar again made me shiver.

"It isn't as if we'd be there alone," Mal pointed out.

"We'll run down and come right back," Stacey promised.

"Okay," I agreed reluctantly. I knew we wouldn't get a bit of work done until I showed them the stone.

When I opened the door to the basement, cold air surrounded us. I shivered again, from a combination of cold and fear. I stepped onto the wooden stair and it creaked. As Stacey and Mal followed, the creaking became magnified. At the bottom, I paused, summoning my nerve before I looked at the corner where the gray stone lay.

Andy and another workman were across the room from the "grave." They looked up as we entered the cellar, looked at one another, then turned back to the wires hanging out of the wall.

"Over there." I pointed.

Stacey stepped around me and stood staring

at the stone in the floor. Mal joined her, and I brought up the rear.

"Cool," said Stacey.

"It does look sort of like a headstone," said Mal. "And think about it. There's a stone floor down here. It would be easy to pry up the stones and then dig in the dirt underneath."

"Stop it, Mal," I said. I looked over my shoulder. The workmen's bright lights were burning in their corner, but the area where we stood was in shadows. It had the musty smell that basements often have, and the walls, also stone, were damp. I doubted that it ever completely dried out down here. "Seen enough? Ready to go back to work?" I asked.

But Stacey wandered around the basement. "I wonder if anyone has searched for the missing Gable papers down here?" she asked.

"It seems like the perfect place to hide something," said Mal.

"Then I'm sure they've already looked down here," I said. I moved to the bottom step and rested my foot on it. "Let's go."

"Wait a minute," said Stacey, stopping in front of what looked like two large black boxes. "Why is a stereo system set up down here? That's really weird."

Mal joined her. "Someone has been playing it," she said. "There's a tape in it."

This was enough to make me step down and have a look.

"Does this belong to one of you?" I asked the workmen.

"Nope. We thought it was kind of strange too," Andy answered. "It won't last long down here."

I punched the PLAY button to see what was on the cassette. In a moment the sound of a beating heart surrounded us.

"The tell-tale heart," whispered Mal.

"Play some real music," Andy said. "That'll put me to sleep." He laughed.

It was the sound Logan and I had heard. It wasn't dripping water — or a living, beating heart. It was a tape. "Where would you find something like this?" I asked, not sure I wanted to know.

"It's probably one of those tapes that parents use to make their baby feel like she's still in the womb," said Mal. "We have one someplace. Mom played it for Claire when she first came home from the hospital."

"You know what this means?" I asked. "This is proof that what's going on here at the store — the raven, the carving, the black cat trapped behind the wall — is a hoax."

"But why?" Stacey asked.

"And who's behind it?" said Mal.

"Too bad we don't have a fingerprint kit,"

Stacey said in a low voice. "We could dust for prints and find out who's handled the tape."

"My brothers have a detective kit," said Mal. "Remember when they were 'secret agents'? The fingerprint powder makes an awful mess, but it sort of works. I don't think it would be enough to convict someone, but you can usually see the prints."

"How would we know whose fingerprints they are?" Stacey asked.

"We'll take samples from everybody," I said, a plan coming together in my mind. "At least, everybody who's here."

"Nobody's here now," Stacey reminded me. "Besides, what are you going to do? Say 'We're playing detective, can we take your fingerprints?' " She giggled. "Then roll their fingers in black ink and put them on a card? Maybe Claudia will take mug shots too."

I laughed. Already I had a better idea. "By the time Mal returns with the fingerprint powder, Ms. Spark and Mr. Cates will probably be back. And the workmen are here now," I said quietly. "I'll make some coffee and serve it. We'll lift the prints off the cups."

"It might work," said Stacey, but she sounded skeptical.

"I'll go home and bring back the fingerprint powder right now," said Mal.

"And I'll make coffee," I said.

"I guess I'll just shelve some more books," said Stacey.

We ran upstairs. I stayed in the kitchen, Mal headed for home, and Stacey headed for the shelves.

"Hi, Mr. Cates, Ms. Spark!" I heard Stacey say. I could tell she was speaking extra loudly, to make sure I could hear.

I heard other voices and stepped into the hall. I couldn't believe my luck. Alex and Mr. Gable! Now we had a chance to check their prints too.

"Someone moved it in here, so there must be a way to move it out," Mr. Gable was saying.

"Hi, Mary Anne," Alex called out.

"Hi. What are you doing?" I asked from the office doorway.

"We want to move this desk out. It wasn't part of the deal when we sold the house," said Mr. Gable. "But we're having a little trouble figuring out how to fit it through the door. I'm thinking it must come apart, because someone had to have moved it in here."

"Maybe they built the house around it," I joked.

"Maybe," mumbled Mr. Gable, measuring the desk with a metal tape measure.

"I'm making coffee," I said. "I'll bring you some."

I returned to the kitchen. A coffeemaker sat

on the counter near the sink. I filled the carafe with water and poured it into the reservoir, then opened cabinets until I found coffee filters and coffee. I measured the coffee carefully. While it brewed, I found mugs, choosing six different colors and designs. I wanted to be able to know whose prints were whose when it was all over.

I found a sugar bowl and a creamer that I filled with milk from the refrigerator. I added spoons to the tray I'd dug up, and arranged the cups carefully around the edges.

"Mary Anne! What are you up to?" Ms. Spark asked.

I hadn't heard her coming, and she almost scared me to death. "Making coffee," I replied. "The weather's so cold and gloomy, it seemed like a good idea."

"You drink coffee?" she asked.

"No, but I thought you might like some."

"Well . . . sure," Ms. Spark said.

"Can I help you, Mary Anne?" Stacey joined us.

"It's almost finished. You can help me serve," I said.

I poured coffee into six cups. "Help yourself," I said to Ms. Spark. "And there's milk and sugar if you need it."

"I'll take it black." She chose a red cup and sipped. "That's good," Ms. Spark said.

Carefully, I carried the tray down the hall. "Mr. Gable, Alex. Coffee?" I offered the tray.

"Just what I need," said Mr. Gable. He took a navy blue cup.

"None for me, thanks," said Alex.

"You've been working so hard," said Stacey. "Come on, we made it special."

"A little, I guess." Alex picked up a cup with flowers on it.

I made a mental note of who'd taken which cup. I hoped I would remember. I also hoped Stacey was noticing too.

Mr. Cates added sugar and milk to his coffee. He drank out of a mug with a New York Yankees logo on it.

I retraced my steps and met the workmen at the top of the basement steps. "Done," they announced.

"Then have a cup of coffee to celebrate," I said, offering the tray.

"Thanks." They took the two remaining cups.

"That hits the spot," Andy said, setting his empty mug on the counter.

The other workman nodded and set his cup beside Andy's, then they left through the back door.

We were alone in the kitchen again. "Professor Kingsolver is the only one who isn't here,"

I said to Stacey. "If the prints on the tape don't match anyone else's, we'll have to find a way to take hers."

"I'm back," said Mal, coming through the back door.

"Do you know how to take the prints?" I asked.

"I had to ask Adam, then promise that I'd do dishes for him, but yes, I know how," said Mal.

"We'll keep Mr. Cates and Ms. Spark busy while you lift the prints off the cassette tape. Those mugs belong to the construction guys. The black one with gold trim was Andy's. The one with the train was the other guy's," I said.

"I have cards for mounting the prints," said Mal.

"We'll have to make sure we're the ones who collect them too," Stacey said. "It won't be much help if there are several sets of prints on each cup."

I carried the tray with me when we went back to the main room. Along the way I collected Mr. Gable's and Alex's cups.

"Is there any more coffee?" Mr. Cates asked.

"Sorry. I gave the last of it to the construction workers," I said.

"Want me to make some more?" Ms. Spark asked.

No! Please don't say yes, I thought. If Ms. Spark came into the kitchen now she'd find Mal and the fingerprint kit.

"Not right now. Thanks, Mary Anne, that was very sweet of you to think of coffee," said Mr. Cates.

I only felt a little guilty as I placed his cup on the tray and returned to the kitchen with it.

Mal was hard at work, spreading powder and lifting the prints with some Scotch tape, then placing them on cards. "We'll have to wash the cups right away, or they'll see the powder and wonder what's going on," she said.

"Did you lift a good print off the cassette?" I asked. That was very important. Without it, we wouldn't have anything to compare the other prints to.

"A very good one," said Mal. "It's clearer than any of the ones from the cups."

"We can compare the prints at the BSC meeting this afternoon," I said.

"And we're going to have to go soon or risk the wrath of Kristy for being late," said Mal.

"We don't want to do that!" I said, laughing. I'd run some soapy water in the sink and as Mal lifted the prints, I washed and rinsed each coffee mug, then put it in the dish drainer to dry.

"Finished!" Mal announced, pulling the last

print, which was from the Yankees mug. She hadn't even taken off her raincoat. And no one had tried to come into the kitchen.

"Where are Tom and Gillian?" I asked when we rejoined Mr. Cates, Ms. Spark, and Stacey in the store.

"They went upstairs to watch television. Cillia is going to cook supper soon. The kids are pretty excited about eating here and not having to go to a restaurant," said Mr. Cates.

"I'd better start if we want to eat at a decent hour," said Ms. Spark.

"Tom and Gillian are also excited about the Sunny Day Festival," said Mr. Cates. "You know, I was pretty lucky to find you guys. You've been great for Tom and Gillian and the store. Now, if Dupin will only figure out what's going on here with the ghost and the raven and the beating heart . . ."

"I'm working on it," I said. And if he only knew what Mal had in her pockets, he might not be so happy about the direction our investigation was taking.

"Time for our BSC meeting," I said to Stacey. "Do you think you'll need us tomorrow?" I asked Mr. Cates.

"If you have time, you might stop by after the festival. We'll probably still be shelving the books."

"See you tomorrow!" I said.

Finding a match to fingerprints is harder than it looks on TV. We spread out all the prints we'd lifted from the mugs. Mary Anne and Stacey marked each card with the name of the person whose prints were on it.

To me, it looked as if the prints could all belong to the same person, but as usual Claudia could see the differences.

Its not that hard. Furst, I made sure I had a good pikture in my mind of the print we wanted to mach. Then, I looked for things that were difrent. Before long I had it narowed to 2. Ms. Sparks was to smal. So was Alexes. That left 4, and thats wen I looked for difrences in desine. I think its this one.

Mr. Cates. Would he set this up in his own bookstore?

I don't think we can accuse him based on the fingerprints. At least, not just the fingerprints. Besides, why would he do it? It could be Mr. Gable. His prints are a pretty close match too.

While the rest of the BSC members were passing the mystery notebook around and writing in it, I noticed that Claudia had cut out the *Stoneybrook News* story about Poe and Co. and stuck it on her bulletin board. *The object of newspapers is to create a sensation*, I thought. And that's exactly what happened when the story appeared. Everybody was talking about Poe and Co.! That sounded like a good enough reason to "haunt" your own bookstore, especially if you'd sunk your entire life savings into it and wanted to make sure there were enough customers.

"Mr. Cates does have a reason to haunt the store," I burst out. "Think of all the attention he received after the newspaper story appeared. So much that he's doubled his efforts to open the store on time," I reminded them. "Publicity — free publicity — is a very good reason to do something. Add that to the similarity in the fingerprints and voilà! We have ourselves a ghost."

"But who cares if he's haunting his own store?" said Abby.

"I don't like the way he's used us," I said.

"Me neither," said Kristy.

"Maybe it's time for another ghost to visit Mr. Cates," I said, busily planning how we could make that happen.

CHAPTER 13

saturday

How do you guarantee the success
of a Sunny Day Festival? Hold it
on the first sunny day in weeks.
After three weeks of solid rain, we
woke up to bright sunshine. The
blue skies and yellow sun were the
perfect cure for everybody's rainy-
day blues.

Kristy's mom and Watson had cleared out their garage and moved the cars to the street.

"Good start to a Sunny Day Festival," Stacey said to Kristy and me when she arrived.

"You sound almost disappointed," said Kristy.

"Not really. But if this is all it took to end the rain, we should have planned the festival two weeks ago."

Mr. Cates pulled up in the Poe and Co. van. Tom and Gillian climbed out of the backseat, Gillian carrying a tray.

Stacey met them at the end of the driveway.

"Where are your sunglasses?" asked Gillian. She wore a pair of hot pink shades and Tom wore aviator-style sunglasses.

"Right here. What's on the tray?" Stacey asked, pulling her white plastic sunglasses with turquoise polka dots out of her pocket and putting them on. They matched her turquoise sundress — which was covered by a denim jacket. Even though it was sunny, it wasn't exactly warm.

"These are our surprise," said Gillian. "Cillia helped us bake them last night." She pulled up the edge of the foil covering and showed a plate heaped high with sunburst cookies. "We used food coloring to make them yellow. I wanted to decorate them with icing, but we didn't have time."

"They look delicious," said Stacey. "Why don't you go set the tray on the picnic table."

"Is this going to be all little kids again?" Tom asked. So far, the Cateses, Karen, Andrew, and David Michael were the only kids who'd arrived.

"I promise there will be boys your age here too," said Stacey.

"Am I late?" Logan asked, coasting up on his bicycle.

"You're just in time to help set up an obstacle course!" Mary Anne yelled from the garage.

"Come on and help me, Tom," said Logan. "Don't leave me alone with all these girls."

Tom adjusted his sunglasses and followed Logan up the drive.

Karen and Gillian were standing in the grass, talking, Gillian talking as much as Karen.

Mal appeared, looking like a mother duck with her ducklings — a line of brothers and sisters — following her.

"What should we do?" asked Mal.

"Go ask Kristy," said Stacey with a grin. "She's the one with a plan."

Kristy was dragging softball equipment out of the garage. "I thought we might practice a little," she said.

"We didn't bring our gloves!" said Margo.

"That's okay. You can use one of these, or you can hit," said Kristy.

Kids started arriving from every direction, all wearing sunglasses.

Claudia brought her face paints and Abby brought a soccer ball. Jessi wore a T-shirt with a huge, shiny gold sun on the front.

Everyone milled around, looking often at the sun as if afraid it might disappear. "Don't you think we should start?" I asked Kristy.

"Ladies and gentlemen!" Kristy yelled. "Welcome to the first and hopefully only BSC Sunny Day Festival."

Everyone cheered and clapped.

"Line up for a parade!" she said. "Hit it, Mary Anne!"

I punched a button on the tape player and a march blared out.

A scraggly line formed as the younger kids marched to the music. Pretty soon, several smaller parades separated from the big line and marched in circles all their own.

"I can't wait to build a sand castle," said Claudia. "Want to help?"

"I think I'll draw something with the chalk on the driveway," Stacey said.

Karen and Gillian were working on a sand castle in Emily Michelle's sandbox. Tom and Byron were tossing a baseball back and forth. Stacey overheard Byron tell Tom that he'd have

163

to try out for his team. The Cates kids finally seemed to be finding their place in Stoney-brook.

Charlotte joined Stacey on the driveway, then Margo and Vanessa wandered over to them.

"I made up a poem in honor of the festival," said Vanessa. "I'm going to copy my poem here." She chose a piece of yellow chalk and printed in big letters:

> Sun is fun,
> Rain is a pain.
> The best thing about a sunny day
> Is going out-of-doors to play.
> Rainy days would be total duds,
> Except for messy, gooey mud.

"Even when the rain goes away, it leaves a lot of mud behind," said David Michael after he'd read the poem.

Stacey sat back on her heels and looked over Kristy's yard. She saw a place where the grass was awfully thin. It was a perfect spot in which to make mud pies. Her fingers itched to dig down in the dark, cool dirt.

"Charlotte, let's practice our cheerleading," Vanessa said. "The Krushers are practicing softball. The first game will be here before you know it."

Charlotte and Vanessa scrambled up off the driveway. As they ran onto the lawn, their shoes squished in the wet grass. From where she sat, Stacey could see speckles of mud up and down their jeans.

In another part of the yard, Abby was kicking the soccer ball to Marilyn and Carolyn Arnold. Marilyn swung her leg back to kick, swung it forward, slipped, and landed on her back. When she stood up, mud reached from her shoulders to her bottom.

Jackie Rodowsky tripped over what looked to Stacey like a blade of grass, and when he stood up, the knees of his jeans and his hands were black with mud.

Everyone playing softball had managed to practice a slide and the mud had worked its way up past legs to arms and chests.

Stacey told me later that she thought maybe it was the most beautiful sight she'd ever seen. Why not take advantage of all the mud, especially since the kids were covered anyway? She called Kristy aside.

"What do you think about mud pies?" Stacey asked in a low voice.

"Messy," said Kristy.

"Could they look any messier?" Stacey asked. "Besides, we're outside."

"Their parents would kill us."

"Would they? Anyway, I don't think mud

pies will make much difference. We can have a mud pie contest. Each person makes one mud pie and decorates it with something they find on the lawn, something that's loose and doesn't have to be picked," said Stacey.

"That might work," said Kristy.

Stacey said she could almost see the gears turning in Kristy's head as she thought it over.

"You'll be in charge?" Kristy asked.

"Sure. I'll make the first mud pie. There's a hose out here that we can use to rinse off hands, isn't there?"

"I'll drag the hose out, but first let's tell the kids." Kristy whistled shrilly. Everyone stopped what they were doing and turned to see what she wanted. Once she got their attention, she turned the stage over to Stacey.

"It's time for the first and hopefully only Sunny Day Festival Mud Pie Contest," Stacey announced. "Each person makes one pie and decorates it with things they find in the yard. The one that looks good enough to eat, wins!"

Stacey led the first group, Byron, Tom, Nicky, and Andrew, to the mud hole she'd chosen. The boys stood over the tempting mud.

"Go ahead," Stacey said.

They stared at the mud, then at Stacey.

"What's wrong?" she asked.

"You go first," said Byron.

Stacey told me later that she was surprised at

their reluctance, since their clothes were mud-covered already. But she didn't hesitate. She stuck her hands into the cool mud. She squeezed it through her fingers, then buried her hands up to her wrists. Finally, she pulled her hands out, cupping enough mud to form into a flat pie in her palms. "Spring," she said, "is finally here."

The boys didn't have to be asked a second time. Soon their hands were as muddy as their shoes.

When parents began to show up, nobody wanted to leave.

Stacey stood proudly over the mud pies while Claudia showed everyone the castles the kids had built in the sand. The driveway looked like a giant rainbow, and only cookie crumbs remained on the refreshment table.

We declared the BSC Sunny Day Festival an unqualified success.

CHAPTER 14

"Are you ready?" I asked Mal and Kristy. They were the only BSC members who had come with me to Poe and Co. after the Sunny Day Festival. We were all tired and still messy from cleaning up after the kids had left, but I was anxious to test my theory that Mr. Cates was behind the hauntings. Inside my backpack were the fingerprint cards, copies of the newspaper stories, and *The Complete Short Stories of Edgar Allan Poe.* In talking things over, we'd decided that Ms. Spark must be part of the scheme too. A woman had bought the raven. Also, Ms. Spark had mentioned that she'd worked in Hollywood, and that her husband had been in special effects. She would know how to make a ghost appear.

We wiped our shoes before we entered the store, trying to scrape off as many layers of mud as possible.

"Doesn't it look fabulous?" Ms. Spark said as we entered.

It did. The first thing we saw when we walked inside was a round table with books arranged on top of it and a big branch sticking out of a vase. It looked like a dead tree — and it was perfect for a mystery-book display. Bright book jackets made the shelves come alive with color. In addition to Claudia's decorations on the wall were posters above the shelves, featuring mystery movies and new mystery-book titles. The floor sparkled, free of loose nails and wood chips. Lenore seemed to reign over it all from her cage at the rear of the room.

"It's a miracle," said Kristy. "I would never have believed the store would be ready so soon."

"It's partly because of all the work you've done," said Ms. Spark.

"I guess there isn't anything else for us to do," said Mal.

"We still need more book reviews for some of the children's mysteries," said Ms. Spark. "I have an empty table saved for a display." She led us to the corner where the children's books were shelved. "If you'll pull the books you want to write about, you can put the recommendations on these cards" (she pointed to a stack of white cards with printed ravens in the corner), "then set them out on the table beside the ones Tom, Gillian, and Kristy have finished. You can arrange a display or I'll do that later.

"I'd also like you to know that we want you to be our very special guests at the grand opening next Friday night," Ms. Spark added.

"Thanks," we said.

I had to wonder whether they'd still want us if my plan worked.

"The kids had a wonderful time at the Sunny Day Festival," said Ms. Spark. "Larry is upstairs helping them scrape off the mud. It was pretty messy, wasn't it?"

I looked down at my own mud-spattered jeans. "It was fun, though," I said.

"You know, the weather can work two ways for a business," Ms. Spark said, looking out the window. "If it's nice, it can mean that people won't mind coming out, but it can also mean they'll have things to do other than shopping. Shopping is something you can do rain or shine. I guess we'll see tomorrow when we open.

"I still have a million last-minute details to take care of, so I'll move out of your way and let you work." Ms. Spark walked back to the front counter.

We each pulled a few books off the shelves and sat down on the floor.

All I wanted to do was spring our trap and see if we caught Mr. Cates. I couldn't think about book reviews.

"Hey, Dupin!" Mr. Cates joined us. "Thanks for the festival. Tom and Gillian are talking about the new friends they made and all the things they did."

"It was fun. I don't think that anyone sees Tom and Gillian as the new kids anymore," said Kristy.

"Well, tomorrow is the big day," Mr. Cates said. "I guess I'll see if the work and planning are going to pay off. But with all the calls we've had since the newspaper stories appeared, I think we'll have customers. I was spending so much time answering the phone that I had to buy an answering machine and make a tape that tells callers we'll open tomorrow morning at ten. Fingers crossed!" He joined Ms. Spark at the front counter.

"Mal, that's your cue — go turn on the tape," I whispered. "If they ask, say you're going to the bathroom or to the kitchen for a drink of water."

Mal stood up and walked slowly past Mr. Cates and Ms. Spark. Neither one said a word as she passed by. She looked at us before entering the hallway, then disappeared.

I waited, my pen poised over the card as if I were going to start writing any minute.

Fluh-dub, fluh-dub, fluh-dub.

I dropped the pen and stood up. "That's it!" I said, turning to Mr. Cates. "That's the sound Logan and I heard when you were gone." I hoped I looked pale. I walked to the desk and grabbed the edge. "It's the ghost. I know it is," I said. "Why is it coming back? What does it want?" I tried to make my voice rise.

Meanwhile, Mal slipped back into the room. "What is it?" she asked in a voice you could barely hear. Kristy joined us at the desk and put her arm around me. It wasn't long before we heard footsteps, and Tom and Gillian ran into the room.

"Dad! What's that noise?" Tom asked.

"It sounds like a beating heart!" said Gillian.

"I'm sure it's water dripping. I'll go check. Everyone stay right here," Mr. Cates said.

Mal had turned the volume up as high as it could go. The beating seemed to surround us.

As soon as I heard Mr. Cates running down the basement stairs, I pulled away from Kristy and started after him.

"Stay here!" Ms. Spark said, coming out from behind the desk. "Let Larry make sure everything is safe."

"I need a drink of water," I said, hurrying past her.

She followed behind me, never quite catching up as I ran down the hall and turned to go into the basement. The sound of the heartbeat stopped as I started down the steps.

"Mary Anne! What are you doing here?" Mr. Cates asked as he started up the stairs.

"Making sure you found the stereo," I said.

Mr. Cates turned a deep red and his shoulders slumped. He looked down at his feet.

"Dad, did you find the stereo finally?" Tom asked, joining us.

"Yes, son, I did. Let me bring it upstairs." Mr. Cates returned to the basement and came back carrying the stereo system. "You and Gillian take this and listen to music for awhile. I need to talk to Mary Anne."

Tom and Gillian ran off with the stereo. The rest of us returned to the front of the store.

"How did you figure it out?" Mr. Cates asked. "You truly are a Dupin."

"For awhile we thought it might be Alex trying to scare you away from the store so he could have the house back, or trying to scare Professor Kingsolver away so he could find any hidden manuscripts before she did. We thought it could have been Professor Kingsolver too, trying to clear the house so she could find Poe's papers or Gable's papers," I said.

"I overheard Andy say that he wished the house would be torn down so there would be some new houses built and more work for his crew, so we thought it could be him as well," I continued. "And we even thought it might really be a ghost."

"For awhile we suspected it might be Tom and Gillian trying to scare you away," Kristy said to Ms. Spark, "but then the tricks became too elaborate."

I pulled the book of Poe short stories out of my bag, then the newspaper, then the fingerprints. "I read 'The Mystery of Marie Rogêt' and was struck by something Poe said, about how newspapers create sensations. That's exactly what happened with this story." I pointed to the feature that had appeared in the *Stoneybrook News.*

"And we remembered Ms. Spark mentioning she worked in Hollywood," said Kristy.

"And Mary Anne said that Ms. Spark was the one who brought up all the strange occurrences when the reporter was here," said Mal.

"I visited the pet store and found out a woman recently bought a raven, a woman who called herself Lenore. Then we found the stereo system and dusted the cassette for fingerprints." I showed Mr. Cates and Ms. Spark the cards. "This one is from the tape, and these are all the suspects. We took the samples off the coffee cups the other day," I admitted.

"I put my entire life savings into this bookstore," said Mr. Cates. "I have to make it a success."

Ms. Spark added, "And when I learned that Poe had visited here, and heard the rumors that he might have done something horrid to Benson Dalton Gable, I came up with the idea of a ghost. But I wanted to make sure that the name Poe was what was associated with the house from now on, not Gable. That's why all the incidents had a Poe connection."

"In other words, the whole thing was a publicity stunt," said Kristy.

"I guess you could say that," said Ms. Spark.

"And you girls figured it out," said Mr. Cates. "That's amazing. I was worried that it would scare off my good workers."

"A mystery only makes us keep coming back," said Mal.

"Until we solve it," I added.

"I hope now that it's solved you won't stop coming," said Mr. Cates. "We still have a grand opening to celebrate."

"I already invited them to be our special guests," said Ms. Spark.

"You know," said Kristy, "maybe you could continue to use the special effects you came up with. That heartbeat would be great as a signal for a door-prize drawing at the grand opening. And the ghost has to make another appearance. The construction worker was the only one who saw him."

"It was dry ice," said Ms. Spark.

"And I guess Lenore will be staying," I said.

"Much to Pluto's enjoyment," said Ms. Spark.

"You wouldn't have to wall up Pluto again, but maybe you could make it sound as if a cat were trapped behind a wall," said Mal.

"I didn't have anything to do with Pluto ending up behind that wall," said Mr. Cates. "He must have wandered back there when the men were working, and fallen asleep or something. I swear that was an accident."

"What about the stone in the basement?" I asked.

"It's a prop I borrowed from a friend," Ms. Spark admitted. "Should we bring it up here or take people on tours of Benson Dalton Gable's grave?" She looked to Kristy.

"The basement," said Kristy, "is much scarier."

"You girls aren't angry, are you?" Mr. Cates asked.

"I was, a little bit, when we first figured it out. But it was kind of fun," I said.

"I'm sorry if I made you feel bad in any way," said Mr. Cates.

"Will you be here on Friday night?" asked Ms. Spark.

"I will," said Kristy.

"Me too," Mal said.

"Dupin at your service," I replied with a very bad French accent.

"Poe and Co. wouldn't be what it is today without Dupin," said Mr. Cates.

"We need to finish the reviews — start the reviews, really," said Mal, "because I have to go home soon."

The three of us wrote several reviews, then arranged the books on the table.

"Where are Tom and Gillian?" Kristy asked. "I'd like to tell them good-bye."

"They came downstairs a little while ago. Maybe they're having a snack," said Ms. Spark, "or they might be in the office with their dad."

As we walked down the hall, I heard Tom and Gillian talking, but not in their dad's office. They were in Benson Dalton Gable's office. The desk that Alex and Mr. Gable had tried to remove earlier in the week was still there too.

"I thought I heard Gillian," Kristy said.

Tom was sitting in a chair on the far side of the desk, writing something. "She's under there." He pointed under the desk.

Kristy and I crawled under the desk, but we couldn't see Gillian. Then I heard her giggle.

"Where are you?" I asked.

A panel slid open, and Gillian and Pluto appeared.

"It's a secret compartment!" said Kristy.

"Let me see," said Mal.

"A big one," I said.

"It's not big enough for Tom," said Gillian, "but it's a perfect secret place for me and Pluto."

"Can we see inside?" I asked. Mal, Kristy, and I crawled out from under the desk. Gillian followed Pluto, who took his time, stretching and sniffing.

"Do you have a flashlight?" I asked Tom.

"In the kitchen," he answered. "Just a minute and I'll be back with it."

"How long have you known about this?" I asked Gillian.

"Not long. I was playing hide-and-seek with Tom a couple of days ago, and I crawled under the desk. I scooted a little, and the panel scooted with me. Tom didn't find me until Pluto meowed," she said proudly.

When Tom brought the flashlight back, I shined it all around the compartment. The only things inside were cobwebs. I don't know what we'd expected to find, but it was a little disappointing to find nothing. The drawers weren't as deep as the space between the two sides of the desk; that's what formed the empty space.

I turned around and knocked on the other side. It sounded hollow too. "Have you checked to see if there's a compartment here?" I asked Gillian.

"Even I don't fit in it," she said.

"So there is a compartment?" asked Kristy.

"Sure, but there's stuff in it."

I slowly slid the panel open. There was a series of dust-covered shelves, and pushed into the back corner of one of the shelves was a small wooden box with a slanted top. I pulled it out and set it on top of Benson Dalton Gable's big desk.

"You'd better go find your dad and bring him here," I said to Tom and Gillian.

CHAPTER 15

"It's a lap desk," I explained to Logan, showing him what we'd found in the secret compartment of Benson Dalton Gable's desk. "It belonged to Gable, and he left some of his papers inside it."

We were at the grand opening of Poe and Co., along with almost everybody in Stoneybrook. We'd been helping out by giving "Poe" tours all afternoon and this was the first chance I'd had to show the desk to Logan.

Logan moved on a little farther. Displayed in a glass case were the letters from Edgar Allan Poe to Benson Dalton Gable that we'd found inside the lap desk. Alex hadn't moved away from the case for a single minute during the afternoon. He was answering questions from customers about Gable. There had been so many, Mr. Cates asked him to stay. And Alex loved it.

"Hi, Dupin," he said, smiling.

"Did the letters in the desk answer all your questions?" I asked him. I hadn't had a chance to talk to Alex since we'd found the papers on Saturday. I knew that Mr. Cates had called Mr. Gable immediately.

"Not all of them," said Alex. "Edgar Allan Poe only visited here once, and Gable was very ill at the time. In his letters, Poe promises to visit again, but evidently Gable died before that happened."

Alex was much nicer now that he wasn't trying to prove a point.

"Looking at his words written in his hand gives me chills," said Professor Kingsolver, joining us. She'd been the one to authenticate the handwriting as Edgar Allan Poe's.

"Were you a little disappointed to find out that there was no quarrel between the two men? No competition or jealousy?" asked Logan.

"I wasn't disappointed at that, but I do wish that Poe had seen fit to leave one small, undiscovered manuscript for us to find," said Professor Kingsolver, smiling. "The letters will do, however."

"We still don't know where the body is buried," Alex said.

He spoke the truth. There was no clue in the

letters and papers to lead anyone to Benson Dalton Gable's grave. It was mysterious indeed.

"But the journal gives us enough material to finally publish Gable's papers," said Alex.

"And they have graciously asked me to help them edit the papers," said Ms. Kingsolver. "It's truly an honor."

Alex rolled his eyes.

"Hi, Mary Anne. Hi, Mary Anne's boyfriend," Gillian greeted Logan and me, giggling again.

"Hi, Gillian." Logan pulled one of her braids, setting off another storm of giggles.

"Your dad's bookstore is doing great," I said.

"And guess what?" Tom joined us.

"What?" I asked.

"Mom might come for a visit, now that we're settled." He grinned a huge grin.

"She called us and said she missed us a lot," said Gillian, looking a little more serious.

"We want you and Kristy and all the baby-sitters to come to a party when she visits," said Tom. "Dad said we could have a party."

Just then I heard it — fluh-dub, fluh-dub. Professor Kingsolver turned pale. I guess we should have warned her.

"Time for the final door prize of the day." Ms. Spark's voice came over the loudspeaker that had been installed for the grand opening.

"This one is a deluxe volume of *The Complete Edgar Allan Poe*."

"I have to go draw the name," Gillian said, running to join Ms. Spark.

"She's going to stay and work at the bookstore," said Tom.

"Who?" I asked.

"Cillia."

Tom didn't look ecstatic about the idea, but he didn't look upset either. I guess that was an improvement.

"Mary Anne Spier is the winner!" Ms. Spark announced.

Logan gave me a little push forward.

I didn't even remember entering the drawing for a door prize. I walked to the front of the store, trying not to think about all the people watching me. My face was flaming.

Ms. Spark handed me a hardcover copy of the book, then gave me a hug. When she let go, Mr. Cates hugged me.

"Thanks," I said.

"You're welcome," said Mr. Cates. "Thank you for all you've done to make the store a success. And I think it will be a success."

"The cash register is smoking, our sales are so hot," said Ms. Spark. She put her arms around Mr. Cates and they hugged.

I thought I might cry, I was so happy for everyone.

The crowd thinned until I was the only one left besides the Cateses. Dad was late for some reason.

"You'll be here to baby-sit on Tuesday, right?" asked Gillian, holding my hand as I watched out the window for my dad.

"I will," I promised.

"Come on, kids, let's go upstairs," said Mr. Cates. "I need to put my feet up."

"I do too," said Gillian.

"Is it okay if I take this book with me?" Tom asked, holding up a copy of *View from the Cherry Tree* by Willo Davis Roberts.

"Of course," said Mr. Cates.

"See you, Mary Anne," said Tom.

"Good night," I answered. I heard a car stop out front. "My dad's here," I added. "See you next week. And thanks for the book." I still thought that last drawing might have been rigged. I did not remember signing up for it.

I heard the lock click behind me as I ran to the car. The lights inside went out as Dad turned the car around. As we pulled into the street I looked back over my shoulder.

Fluh-dub, fluh-dub, fluh-dub. The sound of my own heart beating filled my ears again. I'd swear I had seen the tall, white form of a man, shimmering in the darkness over Benson Dalton Gable's lap desk.

Author's Note

Although Edgar Allan Poe was a real person,
Benson Dalton Gable and his dealings with Poe
are fictional.

If you would like to read more about Poe, check
your local library for his stories and accounts of his
interesting life.

L. GODWIN

Ann M. Martin

About the Author

ANN MATTHEWS MARTIN was born on August 12, 1955. She grew up in Princeton, NJ, with her parents and her younger sister, Jane.

Although Ann used to be a teacher and then an editor of children's books, she's now a full-time writer. She gets ideas for her books from many different places. Some are based on personal experiences. Others are based on childhood memories and feelings. Many are written about contemporary problems or events.

All of Ann's characters, even the members of the Baby-sitters Club, are made up. (So is Stoneybrook.) But many of her characters are based on real people. Sometimes Ann names her characters after people she knows; other times she chooses names she likes.

In addition to the Baby-sitters Club books, Ann Martin has written many other books for children. Her favorite is *Ten Kids, No Pets* because she loves big families and she loves animals. Her favorite Baby-sitters Club book is *Kristy's Big Day*. (By the way, Kristy is her favorite baby-sitter!)

Ann M. Martin now lives in New York with her cats, Gussie and Woody. Her hobbies are reading, sewing, and needlework — especially making clothes for children.

THE BABY-SITTERS CLUB

Look for Mystery #35

ABBY AND THE NOTORIOUS
NEIGHBOR

I heard a familiar sound from the backyard. *Snick, snick. Snick, snick.* Was Mr. Finch trimming his grass again, already?

I moved to the other window and raised the shade. That window has no window seat, so I pulled my desk chair over in order to be comfortable. Then I raised the binoculars and looked.

The *snicking* sound wasn't coming from Mr. Finch's house, after all. It was Ms. Fielding, our other backyard neighbor. She was out there in her big straw hat, pruning her prize rosebushes, the ones she fusses over all summer long. She feeds them and waters them and picks bugs off them and, if you ever start a conversation with her, talks your ear off about them.

I swung the binoculars around, checking Mr.

Finch's backyard, just for kicks. I was a little surprised to see him lying in a lounge chair, relaxing. It seemed early for him to be home from work, but for all I knew he was always home that early. I'd never even glanced at his yard in the afternoon before. I was a little annoyed, too. Why couldn't he be mowing his lawn now, instead of at the crack of dawn?

Maybe he was sick, like me. I focused the binoculars on his face, to get a better look at him.

And that's when it hit me.

That criminal I'd seen on *Mystery Trackers*? The one who looked familiar?

He was the spitting image of Mr. Finch.

But that was ridiculous.

Wasn't it?

Read all the books
about **Mary Anne**
in the Baby-sitters Club series
by Ann M. Martin

THE BABY-SITTERS CLUB®

by Ann M. Martin

Collect and read these exciting BSC Super Specials, Mysteries, and Super Mysteries along with your favorite Baby-sitters Club books!

The Baby-sitters Club books continued...

Available wherever you buy books...or use this order form.

Collect 'em all!

100 (and more) Reasons to Stay Friends Forever!

More titles... ▸

The Baby-sitters Club titles continued...

Available wherever you buy books...or use this order form.

Scholastic Inc., P.O. Box 7502, 2931 E. McCarty Street, Jefferson City, MO 65102

Please send me the books I have checked above. I am enclosing $_____
(please add $2.00 to cover shipping and handling). Send check or money order—
no cash or C.O.D.s please.

Name _____ Birthdate_____

Address _____

City_____ State/Zip _____

BSC997